Happiness

for the

Rancher

Book Four

Small Town

Matchmaker

Cheryl Wright

Copyright

Happiness for the Rancher
(Book Four, Small Town Matchmaker)

Copyright 2023 by Cheryl Wright

Small Town Romance Publications

Dedication

To Margaret Tanner, my very dear friend and fellow author, for her enduring encouragement and friendship.

To Alan, my husband of over forty-eight years, who has been a relentless supporter of my writing and dreams for many years.

To You, my wonderful readers, who encourage me to continue writing these stories. It is such a joy knowing so many of you enjoy reading my stories as much as I love writing them for you.

Table of Contents

Chapter One

Not far outside Crystal Falls, 1880s

Harriet Vogel sat quietly on the stagecoach, her outward appearance not giving away the relentless pounding of her heart.

She glanced across at the other passengers. Not one had spoken to her since their journey began, and she had been traveling for several days. Most of the passengers had only alighted earlier today. The majority of her previous companions had left days before. Harriet was envious.

Fleeing at a moment's notice, she had no plan of where she was heading. Throwing a few clothes and treasured possessions into a carpetbag was the best she could do. Harriet loved her work at the bank and had been there for several years. She was delighted when her loyalty was rewarded with a promotion. Moving from meager bank clerk to manager's assistant was the worst thing that ever happened to her.

Little did Harriet know Mr. Dunning had been embezzling money for years. When he asked her to lock the ledgers into the safe, then left for the day, she couldn't help but take a peek at them. She was certain the bank was doing well, but wanted to see exactly how much they were making.

Heart pounding, she read the figures written in the first ledger. It surely couldn't be right. Then she opened the second ledger Mr. Dunning had handed her. It was identical except the figures were all different.

Harriet sat them side by side, comparing details. The dates were the same, but the figures were completely different. At first, she was confused. Then it hit her—Mr. Dunning was embezzling money from the bank.

She slapped her hands to her mouth in horror. Harriet quickly closed the ledgers and ran to the safe with them. Why had she done that? Now she knew the truth, but what should she do about it?

She was crouched down at the safe she was locking when the bank manager returned. "Miss Vogel," he said, and she turned to face him. A frown marred his face, and then realization hit him. "Why has it taken you so long to lock the ledgers away?" he asked suspiciously, then lurched for her.

It was obvious Mr. Dunning knew she'd discovered his secret, and was out to silence her.

The stagecoach came to a sudden halt. She heard the driver climb down, then move about. Harriet glanced out of the window, checking out the town they'd arrived in. Suddenly, the door opened.

"Crystal Springs," the driver announced. "We will be here for two hours, and two hours only. Anyone who is not back in time will be left behind."

At first, Harriet thought the man was joking. No hint of a smile touched his lips. It could only mean he was serious. He placed the wooden steps at the door, then moved away. He was not interested in helping anyone down the steps, precarious as it was.

Two elderly women stood, then made their way to the door. "Harry Snipes, you get back here and help us down!" one woman demanded. It was clear to Harriet the women were locals. He immediately turned and offered them his hand.

Harry Snipes was an older man and looked tired. He appeared to be in his late forties, and should have retired long ago. At least Harriet thought so. If he couldn't treat his passengers with respect, why was he doing this job?

Once the other passengers had alighted, Harriet stood. The driver glanced up at her impatiently. Was he about to leave her stranded? Harriet hoped not.

Suddenly, he was gone.

"Let me help you, Miss." The stranger offered his hand. From what she saw, his hand was much cleaner than that of the driver. She sighed. Is this what she had been reduced to? Running from town to town, just to ensure her safety.

Harriet clutched her carpetbag and took his proffered hand. He was gentle and his caring voice calmed her fears. She glanced into his face. The stranger was tall and very handsome. She sighed again. Why she was even thinking that way, Harriet didn't know. She was a fugitive and had to keep to herself. "Thank you," she said quietly, but suddenly tripped on her skirts. Why she continued to clutch her carpetbag rather than save herself, Harriet also didn't know, but it's exactly what she did.

Before long, she found herself in the arms of the stranger. Oddly enough, she felt safe. Safer than she'd felt in a very long time. "Oh my goodness," Harriet exclaimed, not knowing which way to look. She felt the heat climb up her face, but had no way of hiding her embarrassment. Had her feet been firmly on the ground, she could have turned away. Held firmly by this man, she was stuck. There was nowhere to run.

When she glanced at him, the stranger was grinning. Grinning! She felt like knocking his hat right off his head. Or slapping him. But Harriet was too much of a lady to do either of those things. Instead, she pursed her lips.

His eyes suddenly opened wide, then he slowly put her to the ground. "I apologize, Miss," he said, his feet shuffling the ground. "You... you were about to hit the ground."

She studied him. That she was, but did that mean he could manhandle her? In this case, Harriet decided it was warranted. Suddenly, the vision of hitting the ground flashed before her eyes. This stranger had saved her from not only falling, but from utter embarrassment. Perhaps even injury.

Without her permission, her hand reached out to shake his. "Harriet Vogel," she said firmly, then wished she'd used a false name. "Pleased to meet you, Sir. I'm very grateful for your help."

His hand clasped around her much smaller hand, and instead of being rough and gripping her hand tightly, he was gentle. "James Owen. Very pleased to have been able to help."

Harriet had an odd feeling about this man. She wasn't sure if it was good or bad, but there was something. Harriet simply couldn't put her finger on it, and instead smiled tentatively. "If it wasn't for you, Mr. Owen, I'd be laying on the ground right now. Most likely, face down." The vision of that didn't appease Harriet, and she flinched.

James Owen studied her. "You've had a fright. It's almost suppertime," he said, pulling out his pocket watch. "I have to eat and so do you. Let me treat you."

Harriet gasped. Should she allow this man to take her for a meal? Even if he saved her from disaster, he was still a stranger. Her heart pounded as she pondered the situation.

"The diner is down the road," he said, pointing toward several stores. "It is public, and I promise you'll be safe. Then I will head home to my ranch, and you will be on your way to wherever you are traveling."

Should she risk it? Harriet had already inadvertently told James Owen her real name. He seemed nice, but so did Mr. Dunning, and look what happened there. Although she was wary, Harriet accepted his invitation. After all, she had to eat. "Thank you," she whispered, still clasping her carpetbag and following him along the boardwalk.

He nodded, and she would have missed it had she not been studying his face. "The food there is good," he said. "Not that I go there often. Only when I come to town for supplies, which is only about once a month."

Luck was on her side. Today happened to be his once a month trip. Otherwise, who knew how badly injured she might have been, no thanks to the driver. Harriet shuddered. Did she really want to get back onto that stagecoach with Harry Snipes driving? She only had to think about it momentarily and knew she'd rather not.

Except it wasn't an option. She had no plans for her future, and nowhere to go. She was aimlessly riding the stagecoach until a town appealed. Harriet glanced about. This one looked pretty good compared to most, but should she stay?

Harriet shrugged the thought aside. It was a small town, tiny compared to most of the towns she'd traveled through already. *Easier to find me.* The thought hit her before she could brush it away.

"Here we are," James told her, and opened the door for her to enter.

"Table for two?" the waitress asked as they entered, a curious expression on her face.

James smiled. "Thanks," but said nothing more. The grin on his face told Harriet he knew the waitress was curious about her, but he had no intention of enlightening her. It was all she could do not to chuckle.

He pulled out her chair and ensured she was comfortably seated. It made Harriet realize James

Owen was a true gentleman. "Thank you," she whispered. If she didn't know better, Harriet would think she was being courted.

Chapter Two

Once their meals arrived, James sat waiting for Harriet to begin eating. She glanced up at him when he didn't start. "You're not eating?" she asked, and he realized she'd never been treated the way a lady should be.

"Ladies first," he said, his fork hovering over his meal.

She smiled tentatively, then carefully took a mouthful of food. For a minute there, he wasn't convinced she would even eat. She seemed— flighty. Scared of her own shadow. It had been a very long time since James had taken a lady to supper. Or any meal, for that matter. But none had acted this way.

Unfortunately, his wife had been gone for a little over four years now. They were long, sad years, but there was nothing he could do about it. His life had changed completely when she'd contracted pneumonia and died.

"It's good," she said, then took another mouthful.

James couldn't help but smile. "The food is good here. How long since you last ate?" he asked cautiously, afraid he might offend her.

She laid her cutlery down and closed her eyes for mere seconds. "Maybe yesterday? I'm not certain."

He couldn't withhold his gasp, and her head shot up at the sound. Suddenly Harriet stood, then shoved back her chair. There was no doubt in his mind she was about to flee. Where she would go, he had no idea. "Please," he said gently, "don't go. I didn't mean to offend you."

Tears danced in her eyes, but she blinked them back, and James' heart broke for her. It was blatantly obvious, to him at least, Harriet Vogel was in a difficult situation. What that was, he may never find out.

When supper was over, he walked Harriet back to the stagecoach office. There was still plenty of time, but he didn't want to hold her up. It was a pity she was leaving. He was certain, had his wife still been alive, she would have insisted they take this young woman home and care for her. Anna would have given her some menial jobs to make her feel needed, and talked to her about her troubles.

It struck James that he could do the same thing, but did he want to? The entire situation would be different with another woman in the house, but there was none. It could put Harriet in a precarious position, one she may not be prepared to accept. "Where are you heading?" he asked, still unsure if he would ask her to stay.

She studied him. Far too long for James' liking. "I'm not sure yet." Her voice was quiet, as though she was ashamed of her answer. But he believed her.

Instead of answering, he cocked his head to the side. Harriet Vogel was perplexing. There was clearly far more to her than he'd first thought. Tears swam in her eyes, but again, she blinked them away. He'd seen Anna do it far too many times. Why women were taught to hide their emotions, he would never know.

James glanced about. No one else was around— there was still plenty of time before the stagecoach left for the next stop. "I have no right to ask, I know that," he said, guiding her toward a chair in the stagecoach waiting room. "What are you running from?" The fear on her face told James all he needed to know—Harriet Vogel was on the run. "Is it the law?"

She shook her head vigorously. "The bank manager where I worked. He…" Tears flooded her face, and he wanted to pull Harriet close and comfort her. Only it was completely inappropriate, and he knew it. Instead, he shoved his hands in his pockets, which wasn't easy when he was sitting down.

She took a deep and fortifying breath. "He had two sets of books." She glanced up at him. "Mr. Dunning was stealing money from the bank, and I discovered it. He wants to kill me." Tears flooded her face once more, and still he fought to keep his hands in his pockets. He could hear Anna's voice in his head—do something. She needs protection.

"Do you like children?" he suddenly blurted out, knowing it was his wife pushing him in this direction.

Harriet frowned. "Children?" She shook her head as though trying to clear the cobwebs from her mind. "I don't dislike them." It was clear from the frown on her face she was confused.

James stood. He couldn't take back what he'd said, so he had to push forward. "My housekeeper has decided she's too old to look after my children any longer. I need a nanny."

Her eyes opened wide in astonishment. "Your wife can't look after them?"

He swallowed hard. "My wife is dead. A little over four years ago. I'm desperate," he said. Almost begged. James watched as Harriet considered his offer. "My ranch is out of town. No one will know you're there."

A variety of expressions crossed her face. Of course, it would be a difficult decision for her to make. But was it harder running, for goodness knew how long?

Finally, after licking her lips several times, she stood. He followed her lead. She was far shorter than James and only reached his shoulder. Harriet glanced up and licked her lips again. "I'd like to help you out, but it would put me in a precarious position."

"Of course," he said, trying not to voice his disappointment. "Propriety. I should have thought of that." He hadn't thought it through—desperation would do that to a man.

"Is there any way around it? Do you have a separate cottage? Somewhere nearby I could stay?" Her desperation was clear. She wanted to make this work as much as he did. But how could they do that when he had no way to house her, except in the main homestead?

"I'm sorry," he said. "I should have thought it through. There are plenty of empty rooms in the homestead, but all the smaller cottages are taken up by the cowboys I employ."

She sat down again, this time appearing far more defeated than previously. Hands in her lap, and head low, Harriet didn't say another word. James felt like a heel. He'd gotten her hopes up, only to let her down again. It was blatantly clear she needed protection, but how could he make that happen? His options were limited.

"All aboard," Harry Snipes called. "Stagecoach is leaving in five minutes."

Harriet stood, then headed toward the stagecoach, still clutching her carpetbag. "Thank you for supper," she said quietly. "I'm sorry I couldn't help you further." She climbed up onto the stagecoach as his heart pounded.

He did not know why, but James suddenly felt overcome with sorrow. If he let her leave, he was certain it would be to the young woman's detriment. Anna's voice pounded in his head and told him he had to do something. Anything. No matter what, James knew he had to get Harriet Vogel out of the predicament she found herself in.

He stood frozen to the spot as several other passengers settled themselves inside with barely room for Harriet to sit comfortably. The door stood open, and Harry was about to close it. James hurried over and stared at Harriet.

"Marry me," he said in a rush, his heart pounding as she stared at him in astonishment.

Chapter Three

Harriet studied James Owen.

The man couldn't be serious. They'd only met two hours ago. Before she had time to think about it further, she scurried out of the stagecoach, to the absolute disgust of the passengers she needed to climb over. Tucking their legs back as far as possible, they didn't try to hide their annoyance.

Harry stood impatiently, then slammed the door closed the moment she was out on the boardwalk. "Too late to change your mind," he said gruffly, then climbed up into the driver's seat.

"Your luggage?" James said. His voice was full of despair. Was he worried about her luggage or because he'd changed his mind?

She lifted the carpetbag tightly clutched in her hands. "This is all I have. I had to leave in a rush." Harriet knew she'd been lucky to leave at all. Had she been older, Mr. Dunning might have caught up with her. If that had happened, Harriet was convinced she wouldn't be here now. The thought bothered her.

James pulled her further away from the stagecoach. Seconds later, it moved off. "What happens now?" she asked, unsure about the entire situation. He could be a murderer or a wife beater for all she knew. Anything was possible—she'd learned that firsthand.

Harriet's heart pounded in her head. How did she even know James Owen had children? Or owned a ranch? It could all be a ruse.

"I wonder if the preacher is available to marry us now?" He seemed to talk to himself rather than to Harriet. Without waiting for an answer, he snatched up her carpetbag, then hooked her arm through his and headed toward the church.

Harriet shuddered. Had she jumped from one precarious situation to yet another? She stared up at James Owen. On the surface, he appeared to be a kind man, someone who cared for others. She'd let her guard down, and was caught unawares. Harriet had accepted his offer. Now she questioned if she'd done the right thing. She flicked her tongue against her dry lips. "Are you sure you want to do this?" she asked quietly. "I understand if you've changed your mind." She truly did. Harriet had regrets she could never take back—like reading those ledgers she had no right to look at.

Why she'd done so, Harriet would never know. Why Mr. Dunning had trusted her to put them into the safe, she didn't understand either. Unless he had wanted to be caught, then changed his mind, making Harriet an unwilling accomplice.

Was that what she was—an accomplice to a crime she had no previous knowledge about? An involuntary shiver wracked her entire body.

"Are you cold?" James's voice seemed to come from nowhere, her thoughts elsewhere.

She shook her head, then smiled tentatively. "Just thinking about how Mr. Dunning changed my life. Do you think he…" She didn't finish the sentence, she didn't need to.

"Did it on purpose? You think he was trying to shift the blame to someone else?" James Owen, the man who was about to become her husband, studied her. "The man is despicable. Out of interest, how long had you been working in that position?"

"A few days at most. I'd been promoted. Great promotion—from bank clerk to scapegoat." Harriet felt the color drain from her face. It was now clear her boss had set her up. Perhaps there had been rumblings about his misdoings and he needed to shift the blame. It was the only valid reason she could come up with.

"I can't fix what happened, but I can keep you safe." He stopped outside the church, then reached for her hand. "Worst-case scenario, we have to wait until tomorrow."

Harriet faltered. Wait until tomorrow? She couldn't go to his ranch unless they were married. The last thing she wanted to do was put her reputation in jeopardy. Although Mr. Dunning had already done that. No doubt he was spreading rumors about her to take the heat off himself. He might have even spoken with the sheriff.

The thought sent fury coursing through her veins.

James knocked on the door, pulling her thoughts away from everything else. "James! What can I do for you at this late hour?"

James quickly faced the preacher head on, going on to explain the situation. "It's like this," he said, telling Preacher Clyde Walters the entire story as they were led inside.

"I see," the other man said. "Well then, we should prepare for a wedding." He smiled briefly and Harriet was convinced the preacher did not agree with the hasty wedding despite his agreement to undertake the ceremony.

He led them out a side door and into the church. Stopping along the way, he picked a handful of flowers from his garden and handed them to Harriet. "Flowers for the bride," he said with a smile, and

Harriet wondered if it was a sign from God. A sign that everything was going to be alright.

"Will and Pearl will be excited about the prospect of a mother, I'm sure," the preacher said to James. At least now she had confirmation the children existed, wondering why she had doubted him.

Her husband-to-be swallowed. "They don't know as yet," he said, then put an arm around Harriet. She felt comforted by his presence and wondered if that would always be the case. Harriet hoped so.

"Here we are," the preacher said once they were inside the church. "You stand there, James, and you there, Miss Vogel." Once he'd placed them correctly, the preacher began the ceremony. In what seemed the shortest time, Harriet was Mrs. James Owen. They signed the register, and Harriet knew there was no turning back.

"How are you feeling?" James asked moments after they'd left the church.

The preacher refused payment from James, but accepted a donation for the church. Harriet glanced up at her husband—a man who was proving himself to be kind and generous. It was the first impression she'd had of him, and Harriet did not know why she had ever doubted it. "Shocked. When I arrived in

Crystal Springs, little did I know I'd be married before the sun went down."

James chuckled. "I could say the same. I only came into town to pick up some supplies." He glanced at her carpetbag. "We should get supplies for you as well," he said firmly, then led her toward the mercantile, despite Harriet's objections.

"I really don't need anything," she said, trying to slow herself down. Her new husband was having none of it.

He opened the door to the store and ushered her inside. "There is a section for women's clothing and accessories at the back of the store," he said, and pointed in the right direction. "I'll be there shortly." James turned to the store owner then. "Is my order ready yet, Dennis?" he asked, Harriet overhearing the conversation on her way to the rear of the store.

Harriet was reluctant to purchase anything. She had some money, but not being able to predict the future, was not willing to waste it on clothes. Instead, she pretended to glance through the clothes rack, and would return to the counter empty handed. As she turned, she collided with her husband.

He stared down at her. "I thought by now you would have picked out at least a few gowns," he said, his expression wary, then flicked through the offerings himself. "This one looks good," he said, holding a pale blue gingham gown in front of her. "It should fit you. I think," he added.

Harriet swallowed. Her ruse hadn't worked, and now she was certain he would insist on her buying at least a few gowns. She mentally added up the cost of the gowns and compared it to the meager amount of money she had in her reticule. Harriet could cover the cost, but it wouldn't leave her with a lot of money to spare.

James pulled out three more gowns, certain he'd found the correct size for her, then carried them to the counter. Suddenly he turned his back on the storekeeper, then opened her carpetbag and rummaged through it. Her heart sank. Her new husband was about to discover how very little she possessed. Despite knowing her circumstances, he would surely think poorly of her. "I'll be back shortly," he told Dennis, as he snapped the carpetbag closed again.

Heat made its way up Harriet's face. She couldn't be any more embarrassed if she tried.

It wasn't long before James returned with two nightgowns, a robe, and unmentionables. He also carried two cakes of perfumed soap and a face cloth that appeared to be quite luxurious.

"I can't..." she began, but he cut her off. Harriet was dismayed—she couldn't pay for all this extravagance. It would leave her almost penniless. What if she needed to get away in a hurry?

James placed everything on the counter and pulled her close. "Put everything on my account, Dennis." Then he glanced at Harriet. "My apologies. Dennis Andrews, this is my wife, Harriet." Her husband had a strange expression on his face, and Harriet couldn't quite fathom what it meant.

At the mention of wife, Dennis's face contorted, and his head shot up. "Wife?" he said, closing his eyes momentarily. When James didn't answer, he packed all her new clothes into a large brown paper bag.

"Thank you," James said, taking the bag from the storekeeper. He quickly ushered her out of the door. The moment they were outside, he glanced down at her. "Dennis is the town's self-appointed matchmaker. He won't be thrilled he hadn't been given the chance to find a match for me." He laughed then and headed toward the wagon, which was already packed with supplies. James added his latest purchases and ensured they were secured before helping her up onto the wagon.

His hands around her waist, he lifted her with ease. Harriet's new husband was obviously a man used to manual labor. She wondered what her new life had in store for her.

Chapter Four

With his wife by his side, James stopped at the arch leading onto his property. It was dusk—far later than he'd intended to arrive home. "See that dot in the distance?" he asked Harriet. When she didn't answer, he glanced at her. His bride was sound asleep as she leaned against his shoulder.

And who could blame her? Harriet had been traveling, trying to avoid the man who was apparently trying to frame her. At least that's what she'd told him. James hadn't thought to question her story, as it sounded so plausible. His wife sounded so genuine, and he was certain she was telling the truth.

Besides, Anna wouldn't have come to his mind telling him to marry her if she were a criminal. Would she?

James shook the thought aside. Harriet was no criminal. She didn't have to tell him anything—she could have continued her journey on the stagecoach and not shared anything. With her still sound asleep, he flicked the reins and continued their journey to the homestead. By now, he expected the children would be tucked up in bed. Four-year-old Pearl would certainly be asleep. Will was a different story altogether. That boy believed himself to be a full-grown cowboy—at six.

He couldn't help but chuckle. But being brought up by cowboys, what did he expect? Perhaps having a mother would bring out his child's side. Will was only two when his mother died, and despite Martha Brady coming daily to care for the children and keeping house for him, life had been difficult. For all of them.

It made him wonder what sort of mother Harriet would make. She was a few years younger than James, and by all accounts had never married. Would motherhood come easily to her, or was she one that didn't have a nurturing bone in her body? Her face had softened when he'd mentioned the children, so that was promising. He would have to wait and see.

He brought the wagon to a halt outside the homestead and pulled on the brake. "Harriet," he whispered, running his fingers under her chin, trying to wake her up.

Her eyes fluttered open, and she gasped. "Where…" Suddenly she straightened up and turned to face him, then glanced about. "Oh," she said, then a slow smile came to her lips.

It was the first time he'd seen her smile. No, that wasn't true. When Preacher Walters handed her the flowers, a fleeting smile crossed her face. He'd liked it then, and he liked it now. When Harriet smiled, it transformed her entire appearance. "Wait there," he said, and scurried down from the wagon. He was around to her side in record time. Helping her up, he'd tried to keep his distance. This time, he wasn't sure he could.

When he glanced up, she appeared to be waiting in anticipation. "I think I can manage," she said, her words not fitting her expression.

"Better safe than sorry. Let me help." He reached out and took her hand. It was so soft and gentle, and he couldn't imagine this woman doing harm to anyone. She put one foot to the step and faltered, almost falling to the ground. Except she didn't. He caught his wife and held her in his arms. "I've got you," he whispered, trying to ignore the feelings that tore through him as he clutched her tightly against him.

Reluctantly, he put her to the ground, holding her until she was steady on her feet. "Thank you," she whispered, a small smile tugging at her lips.

What he had been thinking when he asked this virtual stranger to marry him, James didn't know. He knew, however, he was already far too fond of her. That hadn't been his plan. He'd brought her here to protect her. There were empty rooms, and she could stay in one of those. Now he'd spent time with her, things had changed. For James, at least. His initial plan for a marriage of convenience was quickly changing into far more.

Whether Harriet would agree with any of his ideas was another thing entirely.

He glanced down at her, staring into her troubled face. "What now?" she asked, clearly worried about her future.

He indicated the steps to the homestead. "We go inside. Pearl will probably be asleep, but Will isn't one to go quietly." He chuckled then, but she didn't respond. It was then he realized she was nervous—about him, about meeting the children, and about their wedding night. They'd not discussed anything at length and certainly hadn't talked about the status of their marriage. That was on him. "About... tonight," he began, but she put up a hand to stop him.

"I am your wife," she said firmly. "No need to discuss such things." She was deathly pale, so James was certain his bride was scared, no matter what she said.

When they reached the top of the steps, they stood on the porch and he pushed open the door. Without a word, he reached down and picked her up. She was a light-weight, and he held her easily against his chest. She stared into his face. "What are you doing?" she whispered.

"Carrying my wife across the threshold." He strode forward and into the sitting room. Will sat reading a book. At least he was looking at the pictures.

James set Harriet to the floor, then stepped toward his young son.

"Who is this?" Will asked harshly, glancing up at Harriet, and James was convinced the boy believed his father had brought the devil into his home.

Harriet glanced at her new husband, dismay written all over her face. "Hello, Will, I'm…" James cut her off with the lift of a hand. It was clear Will was tired and out of sorts. He didn't want their first contact as mother and son to be memorable in the worst kind of way.

Will closed the book he'd moments ago been reading and ran to James, wrapping his arms tightly around him. His greatest fear now was that Will understood the situation and wasn't happy about it. It was clear his son was tired.

"He refused to go to bed," Mrs. Brady, the housekeeper, told him. She shrugged her shoulders, and James knew she would have tried several times. "Will wanted to wait up for you." She removed the apron she'd been wearing and hung it on a hook in the kitchen.

Mrs. Brady glanced across at Harriet, but didn't say a word. "I'll take him to bed now," she said, then reached for the boy. Will held James even tighter than before.

"It's alright. You go. Thank you for staying late." James knew he should introduce the newcomer, but didn't want to talk in front of Will. Tomorrow, all would be revealed. In the light of day, things would, hopefully, be different. Pearl at least would be happy to have a mama. At least he hoped she would.

With the sun pouring through the window, James stirred. It had been so long since he'd had a woman in his bed, he was startled to find Harriet laying next to him. He wasn't sure what he had expected from his new bride, especially since they'd only met some hours earlier, but true to her promise, she'd given herself to him.

Harriet, although a complete stranger, already had him intrigued. Any other woman would have run a mile. When he'd proposed through the stagecoach door, he was certain she would refuse. To say it shocked him when Harriet accepted was an understatement. Not that he'd done it in jest—he hadn't. He wanted to help her in any way he could. The words were out of his mouth before he could think it through.

In hindsight, he would do it all over again. This was a win for both of them. Harriet, as it would keep her safe from her pursuer, and for James, as it solved the issue of caring for his children. Mrs. Brady had stepped up when he needed it, but it was never meant to be long term. She was in the age-bracket of a grandmother, not a housekeeper, so he shouldn't have been surprised when she had given her resignation.

"Good morning," Harriet whispered as her eyes fluttered open. There was a smile on her face, and his breath whooshed out of his mouth. James had no idea why he'd been concerned about her reaction this morning.

He reached across and pulled her close to himself. It was nice, and he knew Anna would approve. Their children had been motherless for far too long. He'd been lonely and fretting since the moment he'd lost her. He would never forget Anna, nor did he want to, but now his efforts needed to be focused on Harriet.

"How are you feeling this morning?" he asked, worried she was ready to run. She'd been flighty yesterday, and he didn't know how she would proceed. His proposal seemed to settle her somewhat, but James was certain she was still concerned about her safety.

Harriet glanced up at him. "Mmmm," she said. It wasn't what she said, but the way she'd said it, along with the way she lifted her eyebrows. With the children still sound asleep, James knew they still had a bit of time, and leaned in to kiss her enticing lips. She didn't push him away, nor did she stop him when he took things further.

Chapter Five

Harriet drifted back to sleep for a short time, and when she awoke to an empty bed, was sure James had left her to check on the children.

No one had really ever told her what it was like being a wife, but she'd read things, and friends had told her closely kept secrets. She'd been afraid but had known in her heart James would be gentle with her, and he was.

She was far more afraid of the children's reaction to her than her first womanly experience last night. If Will's reaction was anything to go by, today would not be easy. After all, Harriet was an intruder, a newcomer. Someone to take their father's attention away from them.

Will and Pearl had lived here their entire lives. Harriet had arrived to interrupt their well-oiled routine. What they would think about that, she dared not imagine. She heard the noise of running, and since the sound was so quiet, assumed the children were up.

Suddenly, the bedroom door opened, and pandemonium ensued. "Mama!" Pearl shouted as she hurled herself at Harriet and the bed. Tears ran down the little girl's face. Her arms went up around her new mama's neck, and Pearl gripped her.

Will was another story altogether. He stopped running the moment he entered the bedroom. His eyes pierced Harriet, and she knew he would be far more difficult to appease. James stood behind his son, a hand on the boy's back. He gave Will a gentle shove toward Harriet and the bed. With Pearl still wrapped around her, the new wife and mother swiveled to the side of the bed, her eyes never leaving Will. "Hello, Will," she said gently. "We didn't really get to meet properly last night."

Instead of answering, Will crossed his arms and pursed his lips. "Will," James warned. "Manners."

Harriet understood completely. There was no pre-warning, no expectation of James coming home from Crystal Springs with a new wife. Or a mother for the children. She sat on the side of the bed, her heart pounding and her head aching. Had she caused Will so much distress that he was willing to defy his father? From what James had told her, both children were easy to get along with, and well mannered.

Will seemed to have other ideas.

The sound of a door closing had Will running from the room.

"I apologize for my son," James said. "Our son. This is all new to him." And to Harriet. The difference was she was an adult, and Will was a six-year-old child. She would adapt, she had to. "That's Mrs. Brady arriving." With that, Pearl slid down from Harriet's arms and off the bed to join her brother. "It will take time. He doesn't even remember Anna." Harriet's heart broke. Of course, he didn't remember his mother—Will was only two when she died, and Pearl was a baby. Tears pooled in her eyes, but she fought them back. James sat on the bed beside her, his arm around her shoulders comforting her. "Don't take it personally. He'll come around, eventually."

Would he? At six, Will was impressionable. He also seemed stubborn. Hopefully she could get both children to like and trust her, but Harriet knew she had to take it slowly. She couldn't force herself into their lives so suddenly.

That would never do.

James leaned in and kissed her forehead, then left her alone. For that, Harriet was grateful. It was one thing to sleep with her husband, but to have him see her in a state of undress, that would never do.

She retrieved the clothes he'd removed the previous night and put them aside to be laundered. She'd objected when they landed on the floor, but James had merely laughed. Her new clothes still sat in the paper bag, and she retrieved the items she needed today. She closed the bedroom door and quickly dressed. Today she would hang her gowns in the closet. Would this place begin to feel like home then? Harriet really wasn't sure.

"Good morning, Mrs. Owen," the housekeeper said. "Welcome. Sit yourself down at the table, and I'll bring you a nice cup of tea."

Harriet was speechless. She should look after the older woman, not the other way around. After all, she was far younger. Harriet smiled and sat as she was instructed. "Thank you, but I'm sure I can help." She lifted her eyebrows in question, but was waved into her seat.

"Take it easy today. And for a bit. You need to get used to the young'uns and they to you." She poured a mug of tea and placed it in front of Harriet. "Now, Will," she said firmly, and Harriet glanced up to see the small boy scowling. "Remember what I said?"

"Yes, Mrs. Brady," he drawled as he huddled down in his chair.

James glanced across the table at the boy, curiosity written all over his face. Harriet was curious too, but didn't say anything. Will glanced at his father, then tucked into his oats. Pearl ate quietly, taking quick glances at Harriet now and then, a smile on her face.

Pearl, it seemed, was happy about Harriet being here and becoming her mama. Will, clearly, was not.

"I'm working on the back paddock today," James said, glancing at his bride. "Will you be alright?"

"I'm coming with you," Will said firmly, as though he had the final say.

James's eyes slid to Harriet, and then to his son. "Not today, Will. We're mending fences—there's nothing you can do to help."

Harriet gasped. Did that mean Will went out with the cowboys most days? He was only six, a child. Of course, James had been in a difficult situation, but taking a small boy out to do an adult job was not acceptable.

"We'll find some fun things to do here, Will. How does that sound?" She didn't know what it would be, but Harriet vowed she would find something Will would enjoy. She'd had little to do with children over the years, but would learn.

Will pouted, his gaze on Mrs. Brady. Did the woman have some power over the boy? He seemed to follow her instructions. If only he would do that for Harriet.

Mrs. Brady crossed her arms in front of herself and scowled. Will turned to Harriet. "It sounds good,

Ma'am," he said pulling a face. He was obviously unhappy about the entire situation.

"Ma'am?" Harriet asked, dismayed at this turn of events. Things seemed to get worse by the minute. Her new son hated her. That much was clear. "You should call me Ha…"

James interrupted her. "You will address your mama appropriately, Will." James' chair scraped as he pushed it back.

Cold dread flooded her entire body. Harriet stood. "This isn't going to work," she whispered, then ran into the bedroom she'd shared with James the previous night and closed the door. Opening the closet, she packed up her belongings. Those she had brought with her. As much as Harriet wanted to stay, she couldn't live like this. Tearing father and son apart was not what she'd bargained for.

Her husband did not follow on her heels as she'd hoped. She heard not a sound. Silence surrounded her, except for her quiet sobs. She had known from the moment James had proposed this marriage would not be an easy one. They knew nothing about each other, except the little they'd discussed at supper.

There had been something between them, at least on her side. James was just being kind when he proposed—it was as simple as that. She would pack up and leave the moment James could take her back into town.

She wiped the tears from her eyes and snapped the carpetbag closed. Harriet spun around as the bedroom door opened behind her.

Chapter Six

James's heart beat loudly. There was no way he could have predicted his usually placid son would react this way toward Harriet. Will was normally a well-behaved and well-mannered boy. He was surprised by this turn of events.

Mrs. Brady had it all figured out though—Will was jealous. For the past four years, he'd had James all to himself. Well, except for his little sister. And now he didn't. His father had brought home a complete stranger, and his son suddenly had to share James with her.

He might only be six, but the boy was sensitive. James had never seen him assertive like this. Not ever.

"I apologize for Will's unacceptable behavior," he said gently, as he cautiously stepped toward his bride. She was visibly upset, and he didn't blame her. Harriet spun around, making it impossible for him to see her, and he wondered why. It was then he saw the carpetbag sitting on the bed.

"When you have time, please take me into town. I'll get the next stagecoach out." Her shoulders were shaking, and his heart was breaking for her.

"Mrs. Brady and I sat Will down and explained things to him." He heard her gasp. "Not your situation, of course. We've explained you are not going anywhere, and will be here from now on." He moved a little closer, not sure how to proceed. Harriet was clearly distressed. "I've let my foreman know I won't be joining them today. I'll spend the day here. Perhaps tomorrow as well."

Harriet slowly turned to face him. "I am not prepared to tear you and Will apart." A small sob escaped. "I will survive. I need a lift into town, though." Tears flooded her face, and James felt like a heel. Why hadn't he foreseen any of this? Because Will was not a bad boy. He was a sweet, gentle, and caring boy, and always had been.

He reached out and pulled Harriet close. His arms wrapped around her, and she cried against his chest. "Mrs. Brady believes he is feeling threatened." He rubbed circles over her back, trying to comfort his new wife. "I have never seen Will like this. Never."

She glanced up at him, but didn't utter a word. Her eyes said it all. Harriet was willing to sacrifice herself to save his relationship with his son. It only made him care for her more. "I'm still leaving.

Don't try to talk me out of it," she finally said, then tucked her head against his chest again.

James pulled her closer still. If it meant he never returned to work, he would ensure their marriage worked. Not only for Harriet's sake, but for the children. They deserved a true childhood, and he knew it. "I don't want you to leave," he whispered. She didn't respond. "Neither does Pearl. Given time, I'm certain Will's attitude will change."

Suddenly, Harriet pulled away from him. "I doubt it," she said. Her words held no malice, only what she believed to be the truth. "Pearl seems happy enough to have me here." She managed a tentative smile, and James' heart fluttered. He cared far too much for his new wife already—and they'd met only yesterday.

He would have to protect his heart or it would shatter if she did eventually leave. James glanced at the carpetbag sitting on the bed, then placed it in the closet. "Can we forget all this…" he waved an arm about, "and start over. Will feels bad, but I feel even worse. This is entirely my fault. The children had no warning."

"I had no warning," she said, her lips quivering. "Except I'm an adult and Will is a small child."

"Who thinks he's a cowboy," James said, then laughed. Then he stopped, suddenly somber. It was his fault Will thought that way. Taking him out most days to take the pressure off Mrs. Brady had not been his best idea. She tried to warn him, but James wouldn't listen. And now Will was paying for his mistake.

He pulled Harriet back to himself and wiped a stray tear. "We will sort it out, I assure you. Harriet," he said, lifting her chin with his finger. "Promise you will stay another month at least. Give the boy a chance to prove himself."

She stared up at him, her face blank. He was certain Harriet's brain was churning with indecision. Whether or not she stayed was completely her choice. If she opted to leave, he would accept her decision, and help in any way he could.

Finally, she nodded. "A month, and only a month. If the situation hasn't changed by then, I will leave." James could see it was difficult for her, but he had to accept it.

Harriet was a strong woman. There was no doubt. It was clear she was thinking of his children, and not herself. What he wanted for the children was a mother. He hoped they would one day be one big family together.

"Mrs. Brady has a hot cup of tea waiting for you." James reluctantly dropped his hands away. He could stand like this all day, but right now, there were more important things that needed to be done.

Like having Will and Harriet spend time together and getting to know each other.

"I'm sorry," she whispered, then stepped around him and headed for the bathroom. No doubt to wash her face with cold water. James couldn't imagine the pressure she must be under. It wasn't bad enough a criminal bank manager was after her. He'd brought her here for safety, and Harriet felt uncomfortable and unwanted.

He would make it his mission to change all that.

Will sat uncomfortably in the sitting room, no doubt waiting for Harriet to return. The fire was roaring, and normally, it would comfort James, but today there was a sense of foreboding in the room.

James sat himself beside his son, and they waited for his bride to return.

As Harriet came into sight, Will fidgeted. He might only be six-years-old, but Will knew what was right, and what was wrong. His behavior was out of character for him, and now he had to face the consequences.

Harriet stopped at the doorway and glanced across at the pair sitting next to each other. She seemed to size them up, trying to work out how to proceed. Only this wasn't her fault, and it shouldn't be up to her to fix the problem.

Her gaze went to Mrs. Brady, who sat at the dining table. The older woman nodded, and it appeared to provide Harriet with the strength she needed. She closed her eyes momentarily, ran a hand down her skirt, then proceeded toward them.

Will wriggled in his chair for a moment, then climbed down. "I'm sorry," he suddenly wailed, and ran across the room to meet his new mama. Harriet glanced at her husband for mere seconds, then dropped to Will's level. Her arms went up around him, and she held him tight.

Will's head rested on her shoulder, and his arms were around her neck. Tears swam in Harriet's eyes. It had been a stressful morning, but James believed it would be alright now.

Chapter Seven

Harriet's heart was breaking for the little boy wrapped around her. She was certain he didn't have a wicked bone in his body. His remorse seemed genuine, and it hit her in the heart. How could she not forgive her new son?

"It's alright, Will," she said, patting him on the back. "It must have been a shock for you." She felt him nod against her cheek, then his grip loosened and Will pulled back to glance at her.

"Papa said I should show you around the ranch today." His expression turned serious. "Since you live here now, you need to know your way around." Suddenly, he snatched up her hand and pulled Harriet to her feet and toward the door.

James stood then and watched as they headed outside. Pearl ran to him, and he lifted the four-year-old into his arms. "Where are we going, Will?" he asked firmly.

"To the barn first," he answered without looking back. Letting go of her hand, he ran down the front steps and toward the barn. "Are you coming?" he asked Harriet as he turned to face her. The boy was impatient. Surely it was a good sign that he wanted to give her a tour of the ranch? It hadn't been long since she was sure the boy wanted her gone for good.

"I am coming," she said, trying to hold back a smile. "I'm a little slower than you."

She risked a glance at James, who was grinning. "It's a good sign," he told her, by this time catching up with her. He put Pearl to the ground, and she ran ahead of them.

By the time Harriet and James arrived in the barn, Will was standing at one of the stalls, petting the horse. "This is Toby," he said. "He's my horse. Toby is a Paint." Moving to the next stall, which appeared empty, he said, "This horse is Nester. He's Papa's horse."

"I don't think Mama needs to know all their names. Not now, anyway," James said, still grinning. He reached into his pocket and pulled out some carrots, handing them to the children. "All the horses are housed here. Most are out with the workers at the moment." He turned to Will. "Where are we going next?"

Suddenly, Will turned to face Harriet. "Do you know how to ride a horse?" He pierced her with his eyes, and Harriet felt called out.

She was taken aback, but held her ground with the six-year-old. "I don't," she said firmly. "I've always lived in town."

"Moving on," James said as he stared at his son. She was certain he was trying to take Will's attention away from Harriet's lack of riding skills. "Why don't you show Mama our vegetable garden?" The boy's eyes lit up. "Will loves working in the garden," he explained.

Will reached for her hand again and pulled Harriet along with him. It wasn't long before they came to a large vegetable patch behind the house. "Here it is," he said proudly, and Harriet instinctively knew Will had helped work it on more than a few occasions.

"Oh, Will," Harriet said, trying to take an interest, "this is wonderful. You've done brilliantly." She smiled at him, and her heart fluttered. When he wasn't behaving dreadfully toward her, Will was a lovely boy. She only hoped this was the turning point in their relationship.

Instead of answering, Will grinned. Did this mean they would be friends instead of him seeing her as the enemy? Harriet hoped so. Then he put a finger to his mouth, as though he was thinking where to take her next.

"That's probably enough for today," James said. "There's plenty of time to show your mama around. She's not going anywhere."

Will nodded and headed back to the homestead. Harriet hoped this was the beginning of a new start for the pair. There were so many new beginnings happening right now, and she had to learn to adapt.

Pearl and Will ran ahead and entered the house before the adults. James turned to face her. "Everything will be alright now. I'm certain of it," he said, then held her hand.

Harriet took a fortifying breath. "I hope you're right. I will not be responsible for problems between you and Will."

James squeezed her hand. "I appreciate the sentiment," he said firmly, "but Will needs to behave. The strange thing is, he is never like this."

"Mrs. Brady is probably right. Will feels threatened by me." She glanced up at her new husband. "There is no need. I have no intention of stealing you away from your children. That's not how marriage works." Except in this case, there was no love between them, and Harriet knew it. This was a marriage of convenience, with all the benefits.

If James hadn't stumbled upon her at the stage office, Harriet would likely be suffering on the stagecoach right now. She would be at goodness

Cheryl Wright

knew where, wishing for solid ground. "What now?" she asked.

Her husband studied her. "I am taking time off to stay with you and the children. We can get to know each other better." He wiggled his eyebrows, and Harriet felt the heat rise in her cheeks. "Seriously though, a visit to the sheriff's office is in order. We'll appraise him of the situation, and he can take it from there."

Harriet gasped. "What if he arrests me?" Her heart pounded, and Harriet felt lightheaded. She was ready to run, but to where? Besides, she had no means to get away.

She felt James's arms go up around her, then he pulled her close. "Nothing will happen to you. An investigation will ensue, and they will arrest Robert Dunning." His warmth comforted her, and Harriet knew he would do everything in his power to keep her safe. Only moments ago, she'd been ready to run. Now she knew right here in James's arms was where she needed to be.

"Are you coming?" Will asked, his head out of the front door. "Mrs. Brady has a surprise for us." He grinned, then ran back inside.

"Well, if Mrs. Brady has a surprise, we'd better see what it is," James said, dropping his arms from around her. Harriet would rather stay the way they were. She felt comforted standing there with him, although she knew she shouldn't. A marriage of convenience didn't include feeling good when the other person held you that way.

Of course, it worked for them both. For Harriet, she had a change of name, and was hidden from her pursuer. For James, he had someone to look after his children. It was akin to a contract. Each side received a benefit of some sort. That's what she needed to keep in her mind. Theirs was a legal agreement, with each party deriving something from it.

Harriet knew it would bode well for her to remember that.

Chapter Eight

James held tightly to Harriet's hand. He knew he shouldn't, but it had been so long since he'd had a woman by his side. He could hear Anna's voice urging him to make the most of this marriage. James might have planned it to be a marriage of convenience, but it was already turning into something more.

For him, anyway.

When they reached the front door, Harriet stopped. She took another fortifying breath and let it out slowly. He hated she felt… what? He wasn't sure what emotions she was feeling. It was difficult enough for him—James couldn't even imagine how it was for Harriet.

Within a matter of days, she'd been set up, threatened, then to top it all off, he'd proposed marriage. At the time, James believed he was doing the right thing. Not in a million years did he believe Will would take it so badly.

"Are you alright?" he asked Harriet, then brushed back some loose hair from her face. His fingers tingled from the contact, and he was taken aback. Not since Anna had he felt such a reaction to touch. The only explanation was that he had not touched a woman since his wife's death.

Correction—his first wife's death. He was still trying to get his head around this entire situation. Given it was only yesterday he'd met Harriet, James was surprised at the feelings he was already experiencing toward her.

Harriet glanced up at him, her blue eyes opened wide in amazement. Did that mean she felt it, too? James shook himself mentally—it was impossible. He then leaned forward and opened the door, ushering her inside.

Will and Pearl stared at them eagerly, and Mrs. Brady looked like the cat who stole the cream. "We're going on a picnic!" Will told them enthusiastically. "Mrs. Brady made one for us."

James couldn't help but grin. A picnic would do them all good. When he glanced at her, Harriet was smiling. He knew she wanted to make them a family, to have the children accept her, and let them all have happy lives.

What she hadn't expected, and neither had James, was the way Will had reacted. From such a placid child, it was surprising. Thankfully, it was all sorted now. At least, he hoped it was.

"That's very kind of you, Mrs. Brady," Harriet said. Her voice brought him back to reality. James put an arm around his wife and pulled her close to him. Will watched every movement he made.

"Where should we go for this picnic? Any ideas, Will?" James specifically asked his son to ensure he was included in the decision making. He was already feeling left out, so James would make a special effort to ensure it didn't happen again.

Will did what he often did while thinking about something and put a finger to his chin. "We could go down to the stream. I like it there," he said.

It had been so long since they'd gone there, James was surprised Will even remembered. The last time they visited the stream, Anna was still alive. She wasn't long off having Pearl, and was full of life. She eagerly awaited the arrival of their second child. Little did they know less than two months later, she would be gone.

"Sounds good. Should we take our fishing poles?"

Will's eyes lit up. "Yes!" he almost shouted, then ran toward his father, wrapping himself around James's legs. Guilt overcame him. It had been so long since he'd spent any quality time with his children. Grief overwhelming him, James had immersed himself in his work. Mrs. Brady had taken over their welfare, which had helped immensely.

As he grew older, Will insinuated himself into the daily workings of the ranch, but naturally, at his age, there was little he could do. He was an excellent rider and liked to help. One day, he would take over this ranch, and James knew it would be in expert hands.

The next few days would surely prove invaluable in cementing them all as a family.

He glanced up to see Mrs. Brady smiling broadly. The older woman gazed at him and nodded her head. She had, so far, been instrumental in bringing Will back into line, and now was determined to bring the four of them together as a family.

From the moment she stepped inside his homestead, she'd been far more than a housekeeper and nanny. She had been an integral part of the family, and if one didn't know better, you could be forgiven for believing she was the children's grandmother.

"Why don't you get the horse and buggy ready?" Harriet asked. "I'll get the children ready."

James squeezed her hand, then headed toward the barn. With Pearl on Harriet's lap, they would fit comfortably into the buggy. He was excited to see what the day would bring.

With Nester hitched to the buggy, he led the horse outside. More used to being ridden, this would be a pleasant change for the horse. He would especially enjoy exploring the area around the stream. Unless things had changed dramatically over the past four years, the grass there was luscious and plentiful. A horse's dream.

James caressed Nester's face, then went inside to collect his family. A smile came to his face. It had been so long since he'd even dared to think that way. Everything had changed the moment he met Harriet. It was a chance meeting, and if the stagecoach driver hadn't left her to her own devices to step down, they wouldn't be together now. Was it divine intervention? Anna's voice had thundered through his head, telling him to help her. Every step of the way, Anna had been there, and for that he was grateful. But now he had to concentrate on his children, and on Harriet.

"We're ready, Papa!" Will's voice brought his attention back to the here and now. James had never been one to daydream, but lately he'd been woolgathering far too much. If Anna was here, she'd tell him he was overthinking everything. And she would be right.

Mrs. Brady handed him the picnic basket, and Harriet reached for Pearl's hand. "I can carry it, Papa," Will told him, and his small hands wrapped around the handle.

The basket was not light for a six-year-old and he didn't want his son to feel defeated. "Perhaps we can carry it together?" he asked. "It is a little too heavy for me."

Will grinned, and they left the house together. James placed the basket at the back of the buggy, securing it well, then stood behind his independent son while he climbed up onto the buggy. He heard movement behind him and glanced back to see Harriet and Pearl heading toward them. They were a sight. One he wouldn't forget for a very long time.

"Here, let me help," he said, and helped Harriet up, too. As he held her around the waist, a shudder went through him. James did his best to ignore it, but knew ignoring his feelings was never a good thing. Instead of focusing on it, he lifted Pearl and placed her on Harriet's knee. James climbed up and flicked the reins. Warmth filled him at the vision of his entire family next to him.

He was looking forward to their picnic, but more importantly, they would get to know Harriet better, and she would get to know them.

Chapter Nine

Harriet spread the picnic blanket over the spot James had chosen. It was near the stream, but not so close Pearl, or even Will, might fall in. Nester was grazing not far away and had access to the sparkling, clear water and luscious grass. He seemed to enjoy himself.

Pearl sat on the blanket the moment her new mama sat and huddled close. The poor child was starved of motherly love, but so was Will. From what Harriet had noticed so far, the boy behaved like an adult. Emulated the cowboys.

His father explained Will often spent his days out with the cowboys, fixing fences, rounding up cattle, and more. Of course, he wasn't really doing those things, but to Will, he was. It explained a lot.

Spending much of his time with James meant the boy had become close to his father. Harriet's sudden appearance would not have appeased his sense of closeness to his father. One moment, Will was the center of James's attention, and the next, he wasn't. Harriet was the intruder, and she needed to remember that. At least in Will's young mind.

Hopefully, the talk his father and Mrs. Brady had with the boy would smooth things over. Still, her own actions were more likely to bring about change, rather than adults telling him what to do.

"Come here, Will," James called, pulling out two fishing lines. He placed a worm on the hook and set his son up on the bank of the stream. The water was so clear here you could see the fish swimming, and Pearl was excited. Until her father handed her a line. Then she backed away and ran to Harriet.

"It's alright," Harriet said soothingly. "We'll set the picnic out. What do you think?" Four-year-old Pearl nodded her head, then moved in for a hug. Harriet stopped what she was doing and wrapped her arms around the little girl. She could do this all day. Pearl was such a sweet child, and so far, had not once voiced her opposition to Harriet's presence.

Pearl didn't speak much, and Harriet worried about that. Was it simply she had nothing to say, or was there a physical reason? She would keep an eye on Pearl and try to figure it out. She reached into the picnic basket and pulled out some sandwiches. "What else is in here, Pearl?" she asked her little daughter.

The child leaned forward. "Cake!" she said excitedly. "I like cake," she said, her face beaming. Pearl reached in and pulled out a plate with an assortment of cakes. After placing it on the blanket, she rubbed her tummy.

"Sandwiches first, then cake," Harriet cautioned, and Pearl's smile disappeared. "Oh, maybe we can sneak one piece of cake in while the others are fishing," she whispered, and handed Pearl a cupcake. It was gone in record time.

What sort of mother did she make, spoiling her daughter like this? But Harriet wasn't worried— provided she didn't make a habit of it. She vowed she wouldn't.

"I got one, I got one!" Will's voice was filled with excitement. Pearl ran to find out what all the excitement was about, and Harriet followed on her heels. Her son was beaming, and Harriet couldn't be prouder.

"That is wonderful, Will," Harriet said, although had she been asked, she would prefer not to touch the wiggling creature on the end of the hook. Pearl turned away and buried her face in Harriet's skirts.

"Well done, Son," James said, his face filled with joy. He removed the fish from the hook and added it to a bucket, where it continued to wiggle about.

"Are you ready to eat now, or will you fish a little longer?" Harriet asked. "Pearl and I have set up the picnic."

James glanced at her, then back at Will. "What would you like to do, Son? Are you hungry yet?"

Will glanced from James to Harriet, his smile never fading. It was clear he was proud of himself, and his demeanor had totally changed from when Harriet arrived. She wasn't naïve enough to believe this would be the end of her issues with Will. It was going to take far more work, but especially love.

"Did you have fun today?" Harriet asked the children as they returned to the homestead in the buggy.

Pearl smiled but didn't say a word.

Will grinned. "I caught three big fish today—enough for supper," he said. "I threw a few small ones back," he said, deflated.

James turned to his son. "They will be far bigger next time, and then you'll be able to keep them. As you could see, Will, there are plenty of fish to go around. Taking the smaller fish means we deplete the stream of good-sized fish for the future. Then what will we do?"

Will shrugged. "I guess so," he said, then glanced into the bucket he held between his knees. "Will Mrs. Brady cook these for supper?" He seemed to perk up again at that thought.

"Very likely," James told his son, "but we'll have to scale and clean them first."

The very thought had Harriet's stomach churning, but it was something that had to be done. Would volunteering to help bring her closer to Will? She opened her mouth to offer, then thought better of it. Surely James wouldn't expect her to do such a task? She shivered at the mere thought of it.

The moment the buggy stopped outside the homestead, Will climbed over Harriet and Pearl and ran inside with his bucket of fish.

"Mrs. Brady!" Harriet heard his voice trailing off as he headed into the kitchen, where he would no doubt find the housekeeper. What would he do once the older woman no longer worked there? Would he tell his mother his exciting news? Harriet doubted that would ever be the case, but she really had no clue.

Will seemed to warm to her, but Harriet knew it was going to be a relatively slow process. He'd had four years of being his father's shadow, and now she had forced her way in, effectively pushing Will aside. At least in the six-year-old's eyes. She didn't know how long it would take to earn his trust, but Harriet knew she needed to take it slowly and not try to force him into liking her.

By the time they arrived inside, Will was excitedly telling Mrs. Brady all about their adventures at the stream. "I hope we can go again tomorrow," he said, his excitement clear in his voice.

James stepped forward. Harriet was certain he would say no. She put a hand on his arm, and James paused. Will needed to have this time of happiness. Right now, he was being a six-year-old. Most of the time, he thought he was an adult.

James stared down at her. His nod was almost negligible, but she appreciated his trust in her. The pair stood there, waiting for their son to finish. Pearl stood close to Harriet, her little hands clasped tightly to Harriet's skirts. Glancing down, Harriet knew she had to pay special attention to Pearl as well. The last thing she wanted was to alienate Pearl. She dropped to her knees and hugged the little girl tight.

At least one of her children was accepting of her. It was going to take far longer for Will to endure her in his life. Of that, Harriet had no doubt.

"It looks like we'll be having fish for supper," Mrs. Brady announced.

Will took the bucket from her and headed out to the porch where James and Will would scale and clean the fish, ready for cooking.

Harriet was more than a little relieved she didn't have to take part in that particular task.

Chapter Ten

"That was fun," Will told his father.

James stared at him. "You enjoy cleaning fish?" He chuckled, finding his son's words hard to believe.

Will glanced up at his father and shook his head. "Fishing and having a picnic. This isn't fun," he said, screwing up his face. James couldn't help but laugh.

It was nice spending time with his family. Even better, getting to know Harriet. Never in his wildest dreams did James ever contemplate marrying again. He still couldn't believe he'd done so. Especially after knowing Harriet for only a matter of hours. His heart pounded. Had he really done the right thing?

He had helped Harriet out of a tight spot. At least, that's what she told him. The truth was, his wife could be the one who stole money from the bank, not Robert Dunning. This could be her way of covering up her crime.

James put his grimy hands to the back of a nearby chair. The gravity of the situation suddenly hit him. What if Harriet truly was an embezzler? All he had was her side of the story. If it were true, not only had he sheltered a fugitive, but he'd put his children in danger while doing so.

He shook his head to clear away the unwelcome thoughts. Of course, Harriet was not the embezzler. They needed to go into town and talk to sheriff Tommy Garrett. He would know what to do. Not to mention he would have the means to find out the truth.

Whether it was something James wanted to hear was beside the point. He had to learn the truth, no matter how much it hurt.

"Are you sick, Papa?" Will's voice cut through his ramblings, and James stood straighter.

"I'm fine, Son. How are you doing with that fish?" He watched over the boy's shoulder as he masterfully scaled the fish.

"Finished," Will said proudly, then rinsed the fish in the bowl of water sitting nearby.

He was a little too young to use a sharp knife to cut open the fish, so James took over. "Well done," James told him, and Will watched his father's every move. "Supper tonight will be very tasty."

Will beamed, and James wondered why he even doubted Harriet. She seemed to know how to mend the broken fences with Will, and Pearl had taken to her. He finished cleaning the last fish, then headed into the kitchen with their catch.

Mrs. Brady looked down at the cleaned and filleted fish. "That is much better," she said, then placed it in the icebox. "Coffee is ready, and I have milk and cookies for the children."

"Will and I need to clean up, then we'll return. Thank you, Mrs. Brady." He guided his son to the bathroom. "Cookies sound good, don't you think, Will?"

Will grinned. "I love cookies," he said, then hurried back to the kitchen, James close behind him. Harriet was sitting at the dining table waiting for them. She patted the seat next to her and James complied. Pearl sat on the other side of his wife. Will took his place beside his father.

It worried James. Was Will securing his position with his father? Showing Harriet that Will belonged by his father's side, and not Harriet? He hoped not. After the talk he and Mrs. Brady had with the boy, all seemed to be going well. Their trip to the stream seemed to prove he had accepted Harriet as his mother, but the boy now seemed determined.

There was little James could do right now. Will hadn't done anything wrong, nor had harm come to Harriet. He would monitor the situation, and hopefully, it would all work out for the better.

Glancing across at Harriet as they sat side by side on the porch, James reached for her hand.

"The sunset is beautiful," she said, pulling her shawl tighter around her shoulders. "I've never seen one this lovely."

James chuckled. "You're not in the city now," he said. "We have the best of everything out here." It was true. They got the best sunsets, the biggest view of the moon, and all that fresh air. How anyone could abide being stuck in a building all day long, he didn't know. This was the only life he ever wanted.

Born and raised on this ranch, James never wanted to leave.

"You're the best," she said, and he let her words sink in. It was only a matter of hours ago he was lamenting her guilt at embezzling. Now guilt weighed him down.

James squeezed her hand. "We should visit the sheriff's office tomorrow," he said, turning to face her. Harriet nodded. If she was guilty, surely she would not agree to such a thing.

"It's a good idea," she agreed. "It's possible no one is aware of the crime yet. I only found out because Mr. Dunning set me up."

He studied her face in the moonlight. Harriet was truly beautiful, but now she scowled, though only momentarily. Tears swam in her eyes and his heart thudded. How could he, even for a moment, believe his wife capable of anything untoward, let alone stealing money from a bank?

If what she said was true, she'd been elevated to a position she'd not requested, and left with ledgers she'd never seen before. Besides, James had always been an excellent judge of character, and surely would have noticed something amiss if that had been the case?

Instead, he'd been drawn to Harriet. He'd felt compelled to help her, and in doing so was helping himself and his children.

A tear rolled down her cheek, and James wiped it away. He stared into her eyes, mesmerized by her. He leaned forward and kissed her briefly, then ran a thumb across her lips. James' heart thudded.

Deep in his heart, he knew Harriet was guilty of nothing. She was a victim, and he had to help her in any way he could.

He suddenly stood and scooped her up into his arms. Harriet put her arms around his neck, her smile telling him she approved. He strode into the house, closing the door behind him, and headed toward their bedroom.

Everything would be alright. For the children's sake, and Harriet's, it had to be.

Harriet took a long and fortifying breath as she sat next to James on the buggy. They'd left both the children with Mrs. Brady, as their business in town wasn't suitable for young ears. Especially Will, who, being older than Pearl, seemed to take it all in.

As they pulled up outside the sheriff's office, a shudder went through her. Would he arrest her and throw Harriet in jail there and then? Another shudder wracked her slight frame, and she closed her eyes against the vision of what that would be like.

James's arm snaked around her and he pulled her close. "It will be alright. Sheriff Garrett is a reasonable man. He will investigate thoroughly, I'm certain."

Harriet opened her eyes and stared up into her husband's face. She could only hope James was right. There was nothing she could do if he wasn't. If they threw her in a jail cell, there was no way out. "I didn't do anything wrong," she whispered, and James caressed her cheek.

"I believe you," he whispered back. At least now she knew he supported her.

He climbed down off the buggy and helped her down. His hands around her waist sent shivers down her spine. She had been lucky with James. When she had arrived in Crystal Springs for what was meant to be a meal break, little did Harriet know her life would change forever.

"Are you ready?" James asked, his hand on the door to the sheriff's office.

Harriet took another fortifying breath and let it out slowly. She could do this. Especially with her husband by her side supporting her. She stared up at him, then nodded.

James opened the door and ushered her through. Harriet was certain she would trip over her own feet—they didn't seem to move in the usual way.

"Good morning, James." The sheriff's words were full of curiosity.

James spoke before the sheriff had a chance to speak further. "Morning, Sheriff. This is my wife, Harriet. We have a problem."

The sheriff frowned, and ushered the pair into the chairs that sat in front of his desk. He then reached for a notepad. "First of all, I didn't know you'd remarried, James. When did that happen?"

Harriet sat quietly as James relayed her story to the sheriff. He wrote it all down, not missing any details. Then he turned to Harriet. "I need more information about this man, this... Robert Dunning? How long had you worked at the bank? Did you apply for a promotion? Were you aware of the ledgers before that last day?"

The questions came thick and fast, and Harriet's head was spinning. "For goodness' sake, Tommy, give her a moment to answer." James then turned to Harriet. "Are you alright? Do you need a break?"

"My apologies," the sheriff said. "I am thinking aloud. Let me begin again." He put his pencil down and stared at Harriet. "Mrs. Owen, were you expecting the promotion you were given?"

Harriet licked her lips. "Not at all. One minute I was doing my job as clerk, and suddenly I was told to report to the manager's office. I..." She swallowed hard at the memory. "I thought I must have done something wrong and was being sacked." She turned to James, his presence helping her through a difficult situation. "I don't know what happened to his previous assistant. One minute he was there, and then he was gone."

The sheriff's eyebrows suddenly rose. "He was there that day? Never to be seen again?"

Harriet gasped. "He was there until they gave me the promotion, then suddenly he was gone. That was a few days ago. You don't think…?" She felt the color drain out of her face. "Peter is a good man. He has a young family." She couldn't stop the tears that flooded her face at the thought of her predecessor possibly being murdered. Was her imagination running away with her?

Sheriff Garrett stared at her. "Peter? What is his full name? I'll follow up on that."

"Peter," her voice broke then, and Harriet fought back a sob. How could anyone do such a thing? "I… I can't think."

The sheriff walked away from his desk and returned with a glass of water. He handed it to her, and Harriet sipped it. "Thank you," she said, her mind going in many directions. "It starts with H." She was certain it did. "Oh, Peter Harper. That's his name. I do hope he is alright."

"So do I," the sheriff said firmly. "I believe I have enough information to get some answers. James," he said, turning to her husband. "Please look out for your wife. Right now, I do not know how much danger she's in, but I will assume at this point this Robert…" He glanced down at his notes. "…Dunning is dangerous."

Harriet stood carefully, just moments after the sheriff did, followed by her husband. She was already lightheaded, and the last thing she wanted was to swoon. She was not one of those precious wallflowers who swooned at the drop of a hat. No, she was a strong woman who had already forged a life for herself.

And yet, here she stood. Marrying one man to hide from another. A man she knew little about, but was clearly held in high esteem by the citizens of Crystal Springs. James put an arm around her, as though he knew she would be unsteady on her feet. She glanced up at him despite her embarrassment at breaking down in front of not only her husband, but the sheriff—a complete stranger!

It was enough to make her tears flow again, but Harriet blinked them back. Trying to distract herself, she headed for the buggy.

"I thought we would eat before we leave town. Do you feel up to it?" James' voice was gentle. He was proving himself to be everything she'd originally thought from their initial conversation. Was that really only a few days ago?

Harriet swiped at her cheeks and wiped away the last of her tears. "Allow me a moment to compose myself," she said, then hurried ahead of him. Turning into an alleyway, Harriet leaned against the side wall of the sheriff's office and pulled a handkerchief from her reticule. She cleaned herself up and took some fortifying breaths. There was no way to tell how terrible she looked, but there was nothing she could do about it.

She patted her hair, assuring herself she was as well presented as she could be, then stepped back onto the main street.

"There you are," James said, sounding relieved. "I was concerned, and about to come looking for you."

She studied him then. He certainly appeared worried. Harriet hadn't meant to do that to him. "I apologize," she said quietly. "That wasn't my intention. I merely wanted to appear presentable. As your wife, I have no intention of embarrassing you. Or myself for that matter."

"You will never embarrass me. No matter the circumstances." James stepped forward and pulled her close.

Harriet pushed herself away. "Don't make me cry again, please," she whispered, then straightened her shoulders.

James hooked his arm through hers and nodded. "Of course. I understand. Shall we?" They headed toward the diner—the same place James had taken her not two days ago. The place where she felt safe. But only because of the man she'd eventually married. Harriet only hoped she hadn't turned his life upside down for nothing.

Chapter

Twelve

James watched Harriet carefully. She was as white as a ghost, and he couldn't blame her.

She'd seemed fine. Well, not quite fine, but she seemed to cope until the sheriff asked about her colleague, Peter Harper. The thought he may have been murdered by her pursuer rattled her, and James could understand why.

If he was truthful, he was shaken, too. What if Robert Dunning came after her? Not only would Harriet be in danger, but Will and Pearl would be, too. The revelation bothered him.

This wasn't Harriet's fault. Far from it. She warned him there could be danger, and he brushed it aside. Now his children could get caught in the cross-fire.

"James? Where did you go?" Harriet's voice cut through his black thoughts, and James startled.

"Apologies. What did I miss?" he asked.

"The menus have arrived. I thought you might want to look over the options." Harriet seemed to shrink down in her chair, but the color seemed to be coming back into her cheeks.

He took the printed menu from her hands, and their fingers touched. After all the stress and upset of a short time ago, he shivered at the contact. It surprised him, to say the least. James knew he had a soft spot for his wife, but believed it was because of her difficult circumstances. Could it be something more?

"Have you worked out what you want?" he asked as he skimmed the menu. James rarely had anything different from steak and vegetables. It was not something Mrs. Brady often cooked, as the children weren't fans of the meal.

"I was thinking about the chicken pot pie," she said, and smiled briefly.

"Whatever your heart desires," James said, then cringed. It was such a corny thing to say. Before he could decide whether to apologize, their waitress came back to their table. She placed a glass of water in front of each of them, then took their orders.

The moment she left, James reached across the table. "Are you feeling better now?" he asked gently. She'd not had an easy time of it. There were times he wanted to stop the sheriff, but knew it had to happen. At least now there would be an investigation into the bank manager's behavior. Not to mention Peter Harper's sudden exit from the bank. Those sorts of jobs were difficult to attain, and James couldn't see anyone, especially a family man, walking away voluntarily.

"I am, thank you," Harriet told him, but wasn't her cheerful self. As though she noticed his concern, she smiled briefly. "Thank you for today," she whispered. "It was challenging, but it had to be done." She glanced away momentarily, and without looking at him said, "I hope Peter is alright." As she turned back, Harriet closed her eyes, then suddenly opened them.

It made him wonder if she thought the man she'd replaced had discovered the bank manager's secret, too. Perhaps he confronted the man. It may have been his undoing.

"Steak and veg for you, Sir, and chicken pot pie for the lady. Enjoy your meals."

No matter what Tommy discovered, they needed to get on with their lives. Most importantly, he needed to ensure his family was protected.

"Tuck in," he told Harriet, and after saying their thanks for the food, that's exactly what she did.

"You remember my wife, don't you, Dennis?" James couldn't help but stir Dennis up. The matchmaker had missed his opportunity to match James with someone from the town, and was clearly unhappy about it.

"Of course," he said gruffly. "Mrs. Owen."

"We only need a few things today," James said as he perused the aisles, then headed straight to the toys. "I thought we could get a toy each for the children." He pierced her with his stare. "They will be from you, and only you."

Harriet seemed shocked at his words, but nodded her agreement. She picked up a rag doll and held it to her chest. "Pearl will love this, but what about Will? I don't really know what he likes."

James agreed—Will was difficult to buy for. He was far more grown up than his six years. It was then he spotted the perfect toy. "What about this wooden horse?" He handed it to Harriet, and she smiled.

"They are perfect. I'm sure they'll like their gifts." She headed toward the counter, and James was right behind her.

He wanted to buy a gift for Harriet, although James knew she would object. He continued to search anyway. Then he saw it. Perfume. The container was exquisite, but was it a fragrance she would love? There was only one way to find out. "Harriet, do you have a moment?" he asked, and she glanced back over her shoulder.

"What do you have there?" she asked as she came to stand beside him.

He stared down at her and knew the moment she understood. "I don't need perfume. Save your money for important things."

"You are important," he told her. "Besides, I have more money than I know what to do with. Please accept this gift from me. What is your favorite fragrance? Rose? Lavender? Something else?"

He watched as she swallowed. It was clear to James she had never been truly appreciated by anyone. Men, at least, which was a pity. Harriet was special and should be treated accordingly.

"I love lavender," she said cautiously.

Did she think he expected something in return? James reached for the perfume, then leaned in and kissed her cheek. Harriet's cheeks turned bright red. She turned away and strode toward the counter, where she waited for him to join her.

"We will take all these. Thank you, Dennis. Put them on my account." James watched as Dennis added them to his account, then placed the items in a brown paper bag.

"Good day to you both," he said. It sounded grudging to James, but he could be wrong. He felt a twinge of guilt at depriving Dennis of his favorite pastime, matching couples, but was happy with his choice. He wouldn't change her for the world.

Once they were settled in the buggy, Harriet turned to him. "Dennis doesn't like me, does he?"

James laughed. He couldn't help himself. "It's not you. He's annoyed at me for finding a wife without his help. The man is a nuisance to society. One of these days, someone will match him up, and he won't like it."

Harriet smiled then, and warmth flooded him. James knew he'd made the right decision to marry her, even if she was a complete stranger. There was something about her that drew him in. Anna would be pleased with him, James was certain. Once Will came around completely, they would be one big, happy family.

At least, that was his hope.

The drive back home was a quiet one. If it hadn't been for her excitement about giving the children their gifts, Harriet would likely have fallen asleep.

It had been an eventful day, and she didn't know what to make of it. The sheriff seemed convinced something had happened to Peter Harper, and that truly bothered her. Harriet didn't know the man well, except to say hello when she arrived at work, and farewell at the end of the day.

He seemed like a decent man, one who would be law abiding, and report wrongdoing if he witnessed it. Had he threatened to report Robert Dunning for embezzlement? Until now, the thought hadn't crossed her mind.

She had no doubt that's what the sheriff had believed.

Harriet felt James shift his weight next to her. "Do you know how to use a firearm, Harriet?" He stared at her, his eyes full of sorrow.

She gasped. "I… no. No, I don't. Do I need to learn?" Her heart pounded, and she was developing a headache. Harriet stared at her husband as he drove the buggy. Fine lines were showing around his eyes. She hadn't noticed them before, and knew it was her fault. She'd brought so much angst to James and his children. "James," she whispered despite there being no one else around, "I am going to leave." She heard him gasp, then he pulled to the side of the road.

"Why would you do that?" he asked, his voice full of emotion.

Harriet couldn't cope with his sad expression and turned away. "If you turn around and go back into town, we can apply for an annulment. I'll do what I should have done the night we met—continue my journey to another town." Her eyes stung from holding back tears, but Harriet knew it had to be done. "I've put you, all of you, in danger, and I can't live with that." Her voice broke on her last words, and James pulled her close against him. His arms around her comforted Harriet, and she truly didn't want to leave, but she had to do this. She had to ensure Will and Pearl and their father were not put in the line of danger.

"Let the sheriff do his job," James whispered close to her ear. "We will sort this mess out. I promised to help you, and that's what I intend to do."

"You don't have to…" She didn't get the rest of her sentence out, as James covered her lips with his. Not that she was complaining. She felt safe around her husband, and felt comforted whenever he was near.

When his lips left hers, Harriet felt strangely bereft. They'd known each other for such a short time, but already had feelings for her husband. Oh, she didn't believe it was love or anything like it. She did, however, believe those feelings came out of gratitude.

"No more talk of leaving, alright?" James asked. "I want you to stay, and so do the children. We're almost home, so get ready for the onslaught when they see that paper bag." He grinned at her then, and Harriet felt a little more calm.

Whether it was warranted was another thing altogether. For all she knew, Robert Dunning could be waiting for them around the next corner.

It was a relief to Harriet when they arrived home safely. Already she thought of the homestead as home. Where she'd lived previously was just somewhere to sleep. She had never felt particularly at ease there. Perhaps it was because she was alone, with no one to share her thoughts and aspirations with.

James helped her down from the buggy as the front door opened and two excited children came running outside. Will's eyes went straight to the paper bag, and then to his father. There was no smile on his face, and he didn't seem excited. Pearl was the total opposite to her brother, and was clapping her hands and jumping up and down.

"Mama bought a gift for each of you," he told the children, and Harriet's heart pounded. Will's lack of reaction worried her. Would he throw her gift back in her face? James should have said the gift was from him. That way, Will would not be upset right now. Harriet's fear was he would never accept her. She was right to suggest an annulment—her presence had upset the stability of James' family, and it may never be restored while she was there.

The front door opened again, and Mrs. Brady stepped out. Harriet immediately worried they should have bought a gift for the housekeeper too. As if he could read her thoughts, James squeezed her hand, then whispered it wasn't necessary.

"Let's go inside so Mama can give you your gifts," he told the children. Pearl continued to bounce about, and Will's excitement was still contained.

Once inside, Harriet sat on one of the sitting room chairs. She reached into the bag and pulled out Pearl's gift first, since it sat on the top.

The little girl squealed. "I love her," she said, clasping the rag doll to her chest. "Thank you, Mama," she said, hugging Harriet, then hurried to her bedroom to play.

Will stood on the other side of the room, making no effort to go near to Harriet. James put a hand on the boy's back and gave him a gentle shove.

"This is for you, Will," Harriet said, trying to keep her voice steady. It was not the way she felt.

Will stood stock still as she pulled out the toy. Then, seeing the treasure she offered, his eyes opened wide, and he wore the biggest smile she'd seen since he arrived. "Thank you!" he said excitedly, then hesitated. Was he contemplating whether he should hug her like his sister had done? Instead of allowing Will to wallow in uncertainty, Harriet pulled him close and hugged him. Her son didn't pull away. It had to be a positive step in their relationship.

Will glanced up at his father. "Look at this horse, Papa. It's a beauty," he said, and for the first time in days, he sounded truly happy.

"It certainly is," James said. "Why don't you go to your room and play?" He didn't have to say it twice—Will almost ran to his room where all his toys were kept.

Harriet couldn't believe her eyes. James was right—giving each of the children a gift *from her* was a good move. Whether it pulled down the walls between her and Will was another question altogether.

Harriet stood and faced her husband. "You were right. I was surprised at Will's reaction, but had no doubt about Pearl. She had already accepted my presence."

"Our son will come around. He's already close." Harriet was surprised at James' use of the words of *our son*. It was something she needed to get used to—being a mother had not been on her mind, and Harriet hadn't expected to become one for many years to come.

She had to admit though, it gave her a sense of belonging. Now all she had to do was convince Will she meant no harm.

"Coffee?" Mrs. Brady's voice took Harriet away from her musings. "Tea for you, Mrs. Owen?"

"Thank you, yes. And please, call me Harriet." She followed the older woman into the kitchen and helped with the afternoon tea.

"The children will come running as soon as they realize there are *cookies* to be had." Mrs. Brady raised her voice on the word cookies, and sure enough, running could be heard as the children made their way to the kitchen.

"Cookies! Yummy," Pearl said as she slid to a stop. "We helped." Harriet helped her daughter climb into a chair at the table.

Will took his place at the table and waited patiently. "Thank you for the horse, Mama," he told Harriet. "I love it."

Harriet's heart fluttered. Not only had Will acknowledged her, but he'd called her Mama. It was all she could do not to cry. This had to be a turning point in their relationship.

"Drink up your milk," Mrs. Brady said, placing a glass of milk in front of each child. Moments later, she placed a hot beverage in front of the adults. She then joined them all at the table. "I hope you had a pleasant trip into town."

It wasn't exactly fun, not the part where they visited the sheriff, but the rest of their visit was good. "It was lovely, thank you," Harriet replied, and James reached down and squeezed her hand. Only her husband knew how difficult it had been.

"We had a lovely lunch at the diner," he said, "and our drive home was uneventful."

Harriet turned to look at him. Was James as worried about their safety as she was? He wasn't giving anything away.

It was time they sat down and discussed the entire situation.

Chapter Fourteen

James felt Harriet's eyes on him. Not that he'd told her, but he'd stashed a rifle below the seat of the buggy. With the likes of Robert Dunning possibly loitering about, he wasn't taking any chances.

Right now, he had taken time off from work. His employees were more than capable of running the ranch without him, but for how long? He was enjoying spending time with Harriet and the children, but he couldn't do it forever. What sort of example would that be for his children? James knew it would be a terrible example. Especially for young Will, who knew his father worked daily, and what some of that work entailed.

This ranch would go to Will eventually, and he needed the boy to understand hard work was important. Pearl too, but more likely than not, she would end up married in her early twenties. Besides, women did not become ranch hands.

"Eat up," Mrs. Brady said. "The cookies are delicious—the children made them."

Harriet reached for a cookie and took a bite. "Oh, they are delicious," she said. "What wonderful cooks you all are!"

"Can you cook, Mama?" Will asked, and James wondered if it was a loaded question. He watched as Harriet's head shot up.

"I can. Well, not as good as Mrs. Brady, but I have been known to bake a cake or two." She smiled then, and Will grinned.

His son was surprising James with each passing moment. He was beginning to understand the way Will was thinking, and as his fears unraveled one by one, the boy was more accepting. If they could keep things positive, he should come around completely.

James took a bite of the cookie, knowing from experience it would be delicious. He savored the flavors as they exploded in his mouth. "You are excellent cooks," he said, and meant every word.

Harriet sipped at her tea, and Mrs. Brady did the same. Both women kept a watchful eye on Will. James completely understood their reasoning. "I'm going to take the rest of the week off," James suddenly said. He hadn't intended to make the announcement yet, but thought it might settle Will even more. "However, I have things to do, so won't be available the entire time." Will's eyes had lit up, then his expression became sullen at his father's last words. "You do understand, don't you, Will? We'll make some time to spend together, but not today."

"Yes, Papa," Will said, his entire demeanor deflated.

Harriet stared at him, a frown on her face. "I'll explain later," he whispered, hoping the others didn't hear. This was important and involved her. James had no doubt if Will knew what he had planned, he would want to be involved. It wasn't happening.

"Since you can't ride," James said, "we'll go by buggy, but you will eventually need to learn. Living on a ranch, and this far out of town, you never know when you'll need that skill."

Harriet paled. He reached out and touched her shoulder. "I'm not good with animals," she mumbled, and James was certain she believed that.

"By animals, what do you mean?"

Harriet sighed. "I was bitten by a dog once. I still have the scar." She pulled up her sleeve and showed him a long, jagged scar that ran from below her elbow.

"I hope it wasn't rabid," he said, holding back a chuckle. Not that being bitten was funny, but her entire belief that she wasn't good with animals was decided on one incident. A painful one by the look of that scar, but only one nonetheless.

Harriet glared at him. She didn't say a word, but he felt her wrath as though she'd spoken harshly. "I apologize," he said, meaning every word. "I was kidding." She didn't seem to get the joke. "We will take the buggy today, but you need to learn to ride."

He reached for her hand and pulled her toward one of the stalls. "This is Maggie. She is gentle and likes to be patted." He lifted Harriet's hand toward Maggie's face and his wife stiffened. "I promise she won't hurt you."

Maggie sniffed at Harriet's hand. "She's looking for a carrot. Open your hand." Harriet opened her hand, and he placed a piece of raw carrot there. Within moments, it was gone. "See, she didn't hurt you."

"No, she didn't," Harriet said, sounding a little more confident than before.

"Here's some more," James told her, and handed her a few more pieces to give to the horse. "Maggie is going to lead our buggy today."

Harriet stared at him. "Where are we going?" She seemed both surprised and curious.

Maggie snatched up the last of the carrot, and James opened the door to the stall. "I'm going to teach you to shoot. If that fool comes around here, I need to know you can protect yourself."

"I'm more concerned about the children," Harriet whispered.

"Whatever makes you more comfortable. I can't always be here, but you can carry a firearm wherever you go." He lifted her chin to look down into her face. "I strongly believe that man is dangerous. Until we hear from the sheriff about your colleague, we have to assume Dunning killed him."

Harriet stumbled backwards, and he reached for her. His words had been harsh, but James wasn't convinced she understood the reality of what the bank manager was capable of doing to protect himself.

She stared up into his face, then swallowed. "You're right. I didn't want to believe it when the sheriff suggested Mr. Dunning had killed Peter Harper, but I would put nothing past him."

James pulled her close and hugged Harriet, then suddenly pushed her away. "We need to get started." He took Maggie out of her stall and hitched her to the buggy. They walked her out of the stable, then he helped Harriet up.

The last thing he wanted was to have to teach Harriet to shoot, but under the circumstances, her life, and that of their children, could be at stake.

Harriet's heart pounded, and she felt lightheaded. Not the best start to learning to shoot. James had set up a makeshift target at the other end of the back paddock where he'd taken her. She watched as he strode toward her.

"We're all set," he called as he got closer. Harriet nodded, but didn't feel confident about this entire situation. She hated guns with a passion, and didn't want to learn how to use them. Still, Harriet understood completely why her husband wanted her to become competent with them. "We'll start with a Colt," he said when he reached her side. "It won't fit in your skirt pocket, but it's far more accurate and deadly than the smaller Deringer."

The mere thought of it made Harriet shudder. When she accepted the position of working with Robert

Dunning, little did she know she would end up abandoning her life as she knew it. Nor did she think she would be hiding from the man.

James's arm snaked up around her shoulders. "I know it's a lot to take in, but you need to know how to defend yourself—should the need arise." He handed her the Colt and a handful of bullets. "Put those in your pocket for now. First, you need to learn how to hold the gun in a way that's most comfortable for you." He stood behind her and guided her hands to hold it. Harriet was overwhelmed with emotion, but said nothing. She could do this, she knew she could. And frankly, she had no choice. She had put those sweet children in danger, and she couldn't allow them to become a target for her former boss.

"Like this?" she asked, concentrating hard.

"That's right," James said, his voice full of pride. "You're doing well. Keeping both hands on the butt of the gun will give you far more control. When you're ready, we'll add some bullets and you can try it."

Harriet breathed in, then out, then in again. She could do this. If she told herself enough times, she might even believe it. "I'm ready," she said, then wanted to take the words back.

James studied her. "If you're sure?" He didn't sound at all convinced.

"I… I'm sure," she said, feeling a little more confident now. He showed her the correct way to load the bullets, then stood behind Harriet again, his hands supporting hers.

"When you are ready, pull the trigger."

Although still reluctant, Harriet pulled the trigger. She jolted backwards, and one can fell down.

"Well done," James told her, but Harriet was fully aware she would not have hit the can, or anything, had he not been there guiding her. "Let's try again."

She pulled the trigger yet again. And again. Each time, she jolted backwards. Not enough to knock her off her feet, but enough to put her off balance. "I'd like to try it by myself," she said after a few more tries. Whether it was a good decision was yet to be seen.

"If you're sure?" James seemed uncertain. Which was exactly how Harriet felt, but the sooner she learned to shoot, the better. "Let me reset the cans first." He walked away without further comment. When he returned, James handed her some more bullets.

With shaking hands, Harriet loaded them. James's hands locked over hers. "You'll hit nothing while you're shaking so much."

Harriet nodded. Of course, he was right. She stood with her feet apart, the way her husband had shown her. She straightened her back and held her arms rigid. Taking a long fortifying breath, she lined up the gun with one can. You can do this, she told herself, then pulled the trigger.

Not only did she hit the can, she didn't land on her behind. She was certain James standing behind her was the only thing stopping her from falling. Now she knew she was wrong.

"I'm going to try again," she said, believing it to be a fluke she'd hit the can. The next one missed.

"Keep going. It's all good practice." James was reassuring, and that gave her more confidence.

This time, she hit the can again. "Are you certain you've never used a gun before?" James sounded uncertain.

"Oh, I forgot. My father tried to teach me to shoot, but I was young, only eight, I believe. When Mama found out, she was furious. He never did it again."

"Well, as little as that may have been, I believe it has helped. You need practice, but you are going to master this quickly."

Harriet hoped he was right. The sooner she could protect her family, the better.

James checked his pocket watch. "It's getting late. We should return home. We'll come back tomorrow and do it all again."

Of course, he was right. The more practice she had, the better the outcome. "My hope is I won't need it, but better safe than sorry." She emptied the chamber as James watched on. He nodded his approval. Safety must come first, especially when children were involved. Harriet handed over the Colt and the bullets, and James put them away. He then helped her into the buggy.

Not that she couldn't do it herself, because she was certainly capable, but Harriet liked the feel of his hands on her. She knew she shouldn't, particularly since this was supposed to be a marriage of convenience. For Harriet, at least, it was becoming far more than a convenience. It was turning into something special.

She watched as James climbed into the buggy and sat himself next to her. He was certainly a fine specimen of a man, and she was proud to call him her husband. "Ready?" he asked, turning to face her.

"As I'll ever be," Harriet said, then leaned forward and kissed her husband. She wasn't sure what compelled her to do it, but she had no regrets. Apparently, neither did James. His hands quickly went to her cheeks, and he held her there as he returned the kiss.

Harriet leaned into him. Not only did she feel safe around him, but James always made her feel as though she belonged. Never in her adult life had Harriet felt as though she fitted in. With Will coming around, and James making her feel so special, Harriet finally felt as though she belonged somewhere.

She only hoped it lasted. All she needed now was for Robert Dunning to find her and ruin everything.

They returned to the homestead in silence, neither of them mentioning the passionate kiss they had shared a short time ago. Harriet felt invigorated. She wasn't sure if it was the reassurance she could shoot straight and hit her target, or the fact James had returned her kiss.

What made her kiss him in the first place, she didn't know. She'd suddenly felt compelled and went with her heart. Harriet rarely followed her heart, so it was surprising to her. Normally, she followed the rules of society and propriety. Then again, James was her husband. She was allowed to kiss him. Wasn't she?

She shook herself mentally. Of course she was. Although most women let their men make the first move. Harriet knew her time on earth could be short-lived if her former boss caught up with her. She would make the most of it while she could.

Tomorrow, they would return to the back paddock and she would continue to practice. As much as

Mama did not like her learning to shoot as a youngster, it had turned out to be a godsend. She said a silent prayer of thanks to her papa, who had passed while she was still a teenager. Mama had died not long afterwards. Many had said she died of a broken heart.

No matter the cause, it had been a very sad time for Harriet.

Lost in her thoughts, Harriet hadn't realized they'd arrived back home until James spoke. "Are you alright, Harriet?" His voice was full of concern.

She turned to face him. "I was thinking about my parents. It's been such a long time since they passed."

James pulled her close and cradled her in his arms. "I'm very sorry," he said, his arms comforting her. Harriet pulled away. She knew if she stayed there like that, she would become a babbling mess. So much had happened lately, and she was on edge, but she couldn't let it get to her. She especially couldn't let her troubles affect the children. They were, after all, very young. Both Pearl and Will needed to be allowed to be children. The last thing they needed was to carry the burden of their mama's problems.

Suddenly, the front door flew open, and both children came running out. Both were smiling and laughing. Harriet wasn't convinced the reaction was meant for her, but for James. She looked forward to it being for her in the future.

When that happened, she would know she truly belonged.

"Mama!" Pearl called, then hugged Harriet's legs the moment she was down from the buggy. "I missed you, Mama," she said, glancing up at Harriet.

Will stood behind his sister, a grin on his face, but said nothing. When Pearl moved toward her father, Will stepped up to his mother. "I missed you too," Will said, but made no attempt to hug Harriet.

It was a step in the right direction, and it filled James with joy. The expression on Harriet's face told him she, too, was feeling blessed. "I missed you both as well," she told the children. Then suddenly they ran back inside.

Harriet stood staring after them. "That was a bit of a whirlwind," she said, her eyes still trained on the front door. "Do they often do such things?"

"They do," James said, preparing to unhitch the wagon and return Maggie to the barn. It had been a big day, and he was feeling weary, but no matter how tired he felt, his horses always came first. As he turned Maggie to face the barn, Buck Williams, James's foreman, wandered out and took over.

"You rest up," he said. "You've had a big day."

"That we have," James said. Buck was one of the few people who was privy to Harriet's troubles and was monitoring James's family whenever he couldn't be there. "Thanks," he said as Buck took over for him.

Harriet stood at the front door, watching the pair interact, and James knew he would have some explaining to do.

Instead of an explanation, which James knew he owed Harriet, he put an arm around her and led her inside. The children were quietly playing in their rooms, and Mrs. Brady busied herself in the kitchen.

"Why don't you sit down and rest your feet," James said, genuinely concerned for Harriet's health. It had been a big day for him, and he couldn't imagine how exhausted his wife must be feeling right about now.

"I think I will," Harriet said, sounding weary. "I didn't realize how tired I was until I sat down." She stared at him then. "You must be the same."

Harriet was sweet. She was as concerned for him as he was about her. As the days had passed since their marriage, he was getting to know her better. James concluded Harriet was a very caring person. It was something he'd picked up on that first day they'd met, and if he was honest with himself, it was likely the reason he'd felt a connection with her. Well, one of the reasons.

"I won't deny it's been difficult," he said quietly. "I've never had a day like this one before." He grinned then, trying to ease her concerns. Then he reached over and covered her hand with his. "Sheriff Garrett will get to the bottom of it. The best outcome will be if they find Peter Harper alive and well, and he tells us that Robert Dunning is already locked in a jail cell."

Harriet breathed deeply, closing her eyes as she did so. When she opened them, she studied him intently. "He's too cunning for that."

James knew she was right. This was surely not something new for the bank manager—he'd probably been getting away with it for years. Until his assistant discovered the deception.

"Tea for you, Mrs. Owen, and coffee for you," Mrs. Brady said, facing James.

"Please, Mrs. Brady, call me Harriet. And thank you for the tea. It is very much appreciated." Harriet's words brought a smile to the housekeeper's face, and there seemed to be a skip in her step as she headed back to the kitchen. She soon returned with a plate of pound cake.

"Supper won't be much longer, so don't let the children see this," she said, then retreated again.

James grinned. "There are benefits to being an adult," he said, trying to hold back his laughter. "I don't know about you, but I'm famished."

Harriet nodded her agreement. "I'm feeling peckish, too. I hope it doesn't take the edge off my appetite later." She picked up a small piece of cake and nibbled at it. James took a huge bite. "Do you think we are in danger?" Harriet asked quietly, and James knew she wanted him to be frank and honest with her.

His heart pounded. No matter what he said, it was going to upset his wife. "Until the sheriff tells us otherwise, we have to assume that is the case," he said, keeping his voice low so only Harriet could hear.

She straightened her back and rolled her shoulders. "Thank you for being truthful," Harriet said, her expression blank. "The best thing I can do for you and your family is to leave. Do you know when the next stagecoach arrives in Crystal Springs?"

James couldn't believe what he was hearing. He knew what she was trying to do, but leaving solved nothing. It certainly didn't keep her safe. "Harriet," he whispered. "Leaving won't fix this. You will still have a target on your back." James knew his words were harsh, but they had to be said.

"I know, but at least you and the children won't be in harm's way." Tears filled her eyes, and James watched her fight them back. It was clear to him she didn't want to go. Harriet had quickly become a big part of his family, of his life, and his love for her was evident.

That thought gave him pause. When did he realize he was in love with Harriet? Or was it merely worry for her? It went far deeper than that. James lifted her hand to his lips. "Please don't leave. I am falling in love with you."

Harriet's eyes opened wide in surprise. "You are? I have feelings for you too, but I'm not sure whether it's love or something else."

James stood then and pulled her into his arms. "I promise to protect you, no matter what. We need to see this through—you can't live the rest of your life looking over your shoulder."

Harriet nodded against his chest. "I know, but I worry about putting you all in danger. When I accepted your proposal of marriage, I didn't think it through. It seemed like a good way to hide from my problems."

James wiped a tear from her cheek. "I didn't either, but if I had to do it all again, I would still ask you to marry me."

"You would?" Harriet seemed surprised at the revelation. "Even with all the danger I've brought to your family?"

"I definitely would. Anna would never forgive me if I hadn't helped you. Besides, the children adore you. It was a rocky start with Will, but he seems to have accepted you now."

"That wooden horse did the trick. Thank you for doing that." Harriet leaned up and kissed him gently on the lips. His lips tingled with the contact, and he returned her kiss.

"Eeeewwwww!" Will's voice rang across the room. "That's disgusting," he said, and James reluctantly moved back from his wife.

"Nothing disgusting about it, Son," James said firmly. "It's what adults do when they love one another." He stared at Will, and the boy stared back. Then he shrugged his shoulders and turned away. His concentration didn't last for long, and for that, his father was grateful.

"Supper is almost ready," Mrs. Brady said. "You children go and clean up." The distraction was very welcome, and Harriet seemed relieved.

"I need to clean up too," she said, wiping at her eyes. "I must look a mess."

"You look beautiful," James said. "Nothing can take that away from you."

Harriet stared at him for a long moment, then turned away, heading for the bathroom. James knew the danger was real, but had no intention of telling Harriet how truly worried he was. She was already anxious about the situation, especially when it came to the children.

Tomorrow was another day, and they would get her shooting skills up to scratch. Hopefully, the sheriff would have good news about Peter Harper for them. That would be a load off Harriet's mind. Not to mention his own.

Falsifying bank ledgers was one thing, murdering an innocent bystander was a different story altogether.

Chapter Seventeen

Harriet awoke from a deep sleep—the best sleep she'd had in a long time.

Today they would go down to the back paddock again, and she would practice her shooting. Funny how she'd blocked her shooting lessons as a child from her mind. Probably because it was so short-lived. She had never seen Mama so angry. Nor Papa so disappointed. His argument was a woman needed to be able to protect herself. It turns out he was right.

"Good morning," James said, staring into her face. "Did you sleep well?"

She smiled at him, happy he'd convinced her to stay. If she'd left already, where would she be now? Harriet knew she could be sitting on the side of the road in some unknown town. At least here she was warm and comfortable. And loved. "I slept well. And you?"

His smile disappeared. "I had an almost sleepless night. My restlessness came about, I believe, because of your wish to leave." He lifted a hand and caressed her cheek. "You will be safer here, I promise. I won't keep you against your will, and you are free to go anytime. But…"

Harriet closed her eyes, trying to shake the knowledge he was right. "But Robert Dunning will more than likely find me if I continue to run."

"Correct. If it makes you feel any better, we can visit the sheriff's office today, but I doubt he'll have any further information as yet."

Harriet shook her head. James was right—it was too short a time for the sheriff to tell them anything. Instead, she slid to the side of the bed and put her feet to the floor. "Time to get up," she said. As much as she would love to linger in bed with her husband, she felt as though she was not contributing to the household in any way. "I need to make breakfast," she said, and went to stand.

James groaned and snaked an arm around her waist. "Mrs. Brady will do that when she arrives."

"And when Mrs. Brady eventually leaves? What then?" The housekeeper had agreed to stay until there was no longer any threat, but Harriet felt bad for the woman. She certainly wasn't young, but neither was she at death's door.

"Let's not worry about that now. Come and snuggle in with me," he said, wiggling his eyebrows.

Harriet laughed. "You are very single-minded, husband of mine," she told him, then snuggled down under the warm blankets.

Within moments, Pearl was bouncing up onto their bed, followed moments later by Will. "Time to get up," Will said, and Harriet couldn't help but chuckle.

Harriet took a slow breath in and let it out slowly. She loaded the Colt, then lined it up to shoot the cans set up some feet away. "Top right," she said, then pulled the trigger. The nominated can fell to the ground. "Second from the left." Again the correct can fell down.

She was tired. Learning to shoot well was draining, especially when it was crucial she get it right. Otherwise, it could be the difference between life and death, and not necessarily for her. There were children involved, and other innocent bystanders as well. She had no intention of letting them become victims because of her.

"Second row middle," she said, determination in her voice, and pulled the trigger yet again. Once more the correct can fell down.

"Lower your firearm," James commanded, and Harriet did as he said. Then he took it from her hands. "Your shooting is excellent, but I'm concerned. You seem… angry. What's going on?" He unloaded the gun and put the remaining bullets in his pocket.

Harriet stared at him. "I am angry. Robert Dunning has put our children in danger. Not to mention everyone else on this ranch. I know it's not my fault, but the fact I am here—that's definitely my fault."

James held her by the shoulders. "That is not true. It's my fault you are here. I proposed to you, not the other way around. The children are well protected. Buck is looking out for them and Mrs. Brady. Nothing will happen to them." He studied her, and Harriet knew he meant every word. "I love you, Harriet. I will stand by you until the day I die."

His words had her heart pounding. What if her being here brought about his premature death? How could she live with herself then? Harriet knew she couldn't. It couldn't come to that. She had to ensure it didn't.

"That's enough for today," he said. "You look exhausted."

She was exhausted. There was no doubt about it. Mental anguish was the cause, Harriet was certain. There was nothing she'd done physically that would make her tired. It was the worry of what would happen to this beautiful family. What if Robert Dunning found her and murdered her children in an effort to get to her?

Without warning, she closed the gap between herself and James. She gripped him and sobbed. Instead of chastising her as Harriet thought he might, he held her tenderly, and wiped away her tears. "Everything will be alright," he whispered. "You are distressing yourself for nothing."

She dared hope he was right, but Harriet wasn't convinced. Suddenly, she pulled away and straightened her back. She rolled her shoulders, trying to ease the tightness she felt there. "I apologize," she whispered, then turned away. She must look a fright. What must her husband think of her, dissolving into tears like this? "I… I'm not one to cry easily," she whispered. "I don't know why I'm like this lately."

"It's because you're worried. My Anna got like that when she was worried or upset." He reached out and pulled her back to him, cradling Harriet in his arms. "When you're ready, we'll go back to the children. They're sure to take away your sadness."

Harriet knew he was right. Pearl was always cheerful and would lift her spirits in no time. Will? He was far more difficult to predict. Lately, though, things between them were good. "I'm ready now," she said, sounding far more confident than she felt.

As they pulled up in front of the homestead, it was quiet. Too quiet, and Harriet's heart pounded. She felt hollow from the top of her head to her toes. Where were the children? Why hadn't they come out to greet them?

"James," she whispered, tugging at his sleeve. "Something is terribly wrong." The frown he wore told Harriet he was of the same mind.

"Stay here," he told her firmly.

"No way," she told him, equally as forceful. "Give me the Colt and the bullets. I'm coming with you." James stared at her for mere seconds, then met her demands. Harriet loaded the bullets and scurried down off the buggy before James had a chance to help her down.

They quietly climbed the few steps to the front door, but instead of entering, James peeked through the window. Harriet looked over his shoulder. Her worst fears were right in front of her eyes.

Robert Dunning stood in the sitting room, with Mrs. Brady and the children sitting quietly on the chairs, a gun trained on them.

James backed away from the window, taking Harriet with him. His wife had been certain of this outcome, but he had believed her to be worrying for nothing. Now she was proven right.

The man must be demented to take children hostage like this. His breath whooshed out of him, and James knew he had to defend his children before anything terrible happened to them. He had no doubt their abductor was a killer. Backed into a corner, with nowhere to go, his demented mind was capable of anything.

He would do well to remember that.

"You stay put. I'm going in." James was firm in his demands, and Harriet seemed none too pleased.

They had both hoped it wouldn't come to this, and they'd been proven wrong.

"No," Harriet told him. "I am going in. It's me he wants. There is no point in putting everyone in danger. If I go in, it will appease him. I'll convince him to let the others go."

Before he had a chance to respond, Harriet had opened the door and stepped inside. "What are you doing?" she demanded of the hostage taker.

"Ah, Miss Vogel. Or should I say, Mrs. Owen?" His voice sounded like pure evil, and yet, he still addressed her in the correct manner. That alone proved to James the man was deranged.

Harriet took three steps forward and stopped. She held the loaded Colt behind her back, underneath her shawl. "Mr. Dunning," she responded. "What do you want?"

His laugh was more like a cackle, and it cut through James. He had to get his children and housekeeper out of the dangerous situation they were in. Not to mention his wife.

James turned at the sound of a horse approaching. His relief was palpable on seeing the sheriff, but knew the danger was not over. He put a finger to his lips to ensure the man didn't call to him. Sheriff Tommy Garrett came alone, more's the pity, and hunched down as he approached James. "He has my children and housekeeper hostage. Harriet has gone in, against my wishes," James whispered.

"Do you have a back entrance?" the sheriff asked. James explained where it was. "I'll go around there. You stay here and keep an eye on things."

"Did you locate Peter Harper?" James asked, but the sheriff left his side without answering. It worried James even more than he already was.

"Let them leave, and you can do whatever you want with me," he heard Harriet say.

"They stay." Dunning was determined in his response.

"Then I leave," Harriet said firmly.

Pearl began to cry. "Mama, Mama," she said, then jumped up from the chair and ran to Harriet.

"Oh, for goodness' sakes," Dunning said. "Get the brats out of here. I can't stand the noise." He motioned for his hostages to leave, and Mrs. Brady grabbed the children by the hand and led them outside.

"Take them into the barn," James said. It was then he realized Buck wasn't around. "Have you seen Buck?" he asked Mrs. Brady.

"No, but I heard a gunshot before that man stormed into the house." She hurried away with the children toward the barn. James' heart sank. He prayed Buck was not dead. He couldn't live with that guilt, if he was.

Once the children were clear of the house, James' attention went back to Harriet and Dunning. "You ruined my life," Dunning said viciously. "The sheriff came for me. Why did you have to tell?"

"You ruined your own life," Harriet said firmly. "It was you who stole from the bank, not me. It was also you who tried to set me up. What did you do to Peter Harper?" she demanded.

Her question seemed to rattle Dunning, and instead of answering, he cocked his gun with a shaking hand. James watched in horror, his rifle already aimed at the criminal standing in his sitting room.

With lightning speed, Harriet's hand went up, and a shot rang out. Then a second shot rang out. Only this time, Dunning fell to the floor. Harriet appeared shocked.

"I… I only shot once," she said. It was then James noticed the sheriff with his gun trained where Dunning previously stood.

Sheriff Garrett removed Dunning's gun from where it landed and handcuffed him. He checked the man's pulse. "He's still alive," he said. "He'll go to jail for the rest of his life—if the judge doesn't decide to hang him."

Harriet dropped into a chair, and James took the Colt from her hands. "I need to check on Buck. Mrs. Brady heard a gunshot before Dunning stormed inside," he told them. Harriet jumped up and followed him out.

Mrs. Brady was kneeling next to Buck. She'd removed her apron and was holding it to the man's shoulder. "He was passed out when I arrived. He's lost a lot of blood, but should be alright."

Suddenly, the barn seemed full to overflowing. All the remaining workers had arrived at the homestead. Some flowed into the barn, the others stormed the house with guns in hand.

"The danger is over," James told them, "but we need to get Buck to the doc. He's been shot."

It didn't take long before Maggie was hitched to the wagon, and Buck was loaded onto the back. They also loaded the prisoner, with the sheriff standing guard. He knew it wasn't very Christian of him, but James truly didn't care what happened to Dunning. The man had caused harm to many.

As much as James wanted to travel with Buck to town, he wanted to stay with Harriet and the children. Buck said he understood.

The man was amazing. Buck had endeavored to defend the children and was shot for his trouble.

James was truly grateful to Buck, and would ensure he knew it. Harriet joined him out front at the wagon. She still seemed in shock, but she was alive. That was the main thing.

"This is exactly what I was worried about," she said, not showing any emotion. "Are the children alright?" she asked, glancing about, trying to locate them.

"They're rattled, but unharmed. Mrs. Brady has taken them for a stroll." James pulled her close. "I thought I was going to lose you when you stormed the house." His heart pounded at the memory. "I had my rifle trained on him, and then you stepped into my sights. To shoot him, I would have to shoot you."

She glanced up at him. "I'm very pleased you didn't," she said, a tentative smile on her face. "I was more focused on getting the children and Mrs. Brady out. After that, I knew what I had to do."

"And you did it," he said, caressing her cheek. "You are very brave, Harriet. Few women would have done what you did."

"My anger kicked in the moment I saw he had a gun trained on the children and Mrs. Brady. How dare he put my family in danger?" Harriet's voice proved she was still angry. Hopefully, when she calmed down, her anger would dissipate.

"Mama! Papa!" Will's voice rang out across the yard as he ran toward them. Pearl wasn't far behind him.

Harriet dropped to her knees and cradled their children in her arms. "I'm so sorry," she said over and over.

Will pulled back and stared at her. "It wasn't your fault," he said firmly, then hugged Harriet again.

James' heart fluttered at the picture in front of him. He was certain everything would be alright from now on.

Six weeks later…

Harriet sat quietly in the courtroom. Peter Harper was in the witness box.

"The moment I saw those ledgers, I knew I was in danger," he told the court. "I went straight to the sheriff, and he arranged for me and my family to be hidden away until the danger was over." He turned to face Harriet. "I am so sorry my actions put you in danger, Mrs. Owen. That was never my intention."

Harriet nodded. She had been certain that was the case. It was such a relief to find out her colleague was alive and well. Peter continued with his testimony, explaining how he'd discovered the two sets of ledgers, and confronted his boss, who had threatened Peter's family if he made any sort of disclosure. Before the sheriff could do anything, he had been replaced, and Harriet was already on the run.

James reached for her hand and squeezed it. Harriet was glad this day had finally arrived. Sheriff Tommy Garrett told her she didn't have to appear as a witness if she chose not to. With Peter Harper as their star witness, the man would still be convicted, but the penalty would not be as severe.

"Thank you, Mr. Harper. You may now step down."

Harriet watched as Peter returned to his original seat in the courtroom.

"The court calls Mrs. Owen to the stand, Your Honor," the bailiff said, then Harriet swore on the Bible to tell the truth.

"Please tell the court your version of events," the judge ordered.

Harriet took a long fortifying breath and put a hand to her swollen belly. The danger was over, but she still felt as though danger was still present, and she had to protect her unborn baby. "It all started after Peter left the bank," she said. "At least I was told he'd left." Her story spilled out and with every word, Harriet felt relief. She'd been dreading this day, but now it had arrived, she was happy to get it over and done with.

"Thank you, Mrs. Owen. You may step down." The judge nodded at her as though thanking her a second time for relaying her horrific story. "We will take a break, and I will give my verdict. Court is adjourned for one hour," he said, then slammed his gavel.

"All rise."

James held Harriet as the judge left the courtroom. Robert Dunning threw daggers at her with his eyes, and the guard shoved him out of the back door into the Sheriff's office. He would stay in a jail cell until court resumed.

"I'm glad that is over," Harriet said. "I'm not sure I could take much more."

James pulled her close. "You're a strong woman. You can do anything you set your mind to do." He kissed her forehead, and Harriet knew he was right.

"Let's get out of here for a while," James told her. "A nice cup of tea, perhaps?"

Harriet closed her eyes. It had been harrowing relaying her story for all to hear, but it had to be done. Otherwise, Robert Dunning could be set free. Or receive a shorter sentence. The man was capable of anything, including murder, and she wouldn't feel safe with him on the streets.

As they made their way out of the courtroom, they passed Peter Harper. Harriet squeezed James' hand. Perhaps Peter would enjoy a break too. Her husband took the hint. "Would you like to join us at the diner? My treat."

They'd met briefly before the trial began, and he seemed surprised at the invitation. "Thank you, but you don't have to…"

James interrupted him. "You probably need a break, as Harriet does. I can assure you it's no trouble."

"Thank you. Both of you," Peter said, then stood to join them.

Harriet felt the stress leave her shoulders as the three sat quietly in the diner. Peter sipped his coffee and ate the muffins James had ordered. "Giving my testimony was awful," Harriet said. "It's one of the worst things I've ever had to do."

Peter stared at her. "I'm sorry you and your family had to go through that," he said, sounding genuinely apologetic. "I can't tell you how upset I was to find out your children were held hostage."

James studied the other victim of Robert Dunning. "You have nothing to apologize for. That madman will get what he deserves. I've heard this judge can be pretty harsh." He stared at Harriet then. "Let's hope he lives up to his reputation."

They'd not long finished their refreshments when James announced it was time to return. "Why don't you sit with us?" James asked their new friend. "We're all in this together."

Harriet was surprised at his words, but wasn't sure why. James was right. Peter had endured a lot as well. "That we are," she said, hoping to convince him to stay with them. The last thing she would want was to sit alone. It must have been difficult for Peter.

"Thank you both. I accept your offer," he said, then they all stood and returned to the courtroom.

The three sat in the front seat together. The guard returned Robert Dunning to the courtroom and placed him in the dock at the side of the courtroom. On display for all to see. Harriet cringed when he stared at her. His expression made her sink down in her seat. James pulled her closer. "Forget him. The man will be locked away for the rest of his life, however long or short that may be."

She knew her husband was right.

"Exactly," Peter said. "Don't let him intimidate you. He doesn't deserve to live. He tried to kill both of us, and our families," he said. "I have no sympathy for the man."

Harriet knew he was right.

"All rise," the bailiff said, and everyone stood when the judge returned.

"I have deliberated on this case," said Judge Henry Garrison. "And I find the accused guilty of all charges." He shuffled around the papers on his desk, then referred to his notes. "That includes embezzlement, several counts of threat to kill, five counts of attempted murder, and four counts of kidnapping." Harriet's relief was palpable. "I could order you, Robert Dunning, to be hanged, but that's too easy. You will spend the rest of your natural life in jail, with hard labor."

Judge Garrison slammed his gavel, then stood. "Get him out of here," the judge ordered, then left the courtroom without another word.

James put an arm around her and held Harriet tightly. She glanced across at Peter Harper. He seemed to be in shock, as she was. They couldn't have asked for a better outcome.

Epilogue

Two years later...

Pearl sat next to Harriet as she breastfed baby Elsie. Even a few months after the baby arrived, Pearl still seemed in awe. "She's so pretty," Pearl said as she caressed the baby's cheek. James's eldest daughter was talking far better now, and had taken pride in being a big sister.

Little Adam tottered across the room. He was still finding his balance, and his little arms went out to straighten himself. James reached down and picked his youngest son up. Tiny arms circled his neck, and James closed his eyes momentarily. His heart fluttered. Since Harriet's arrival, life was filled with happiness.

Harriet stared up at him. She was beaming.

Will was at the front door, waiting to go outside. "Are you ready, Papa?" he asked. The boy was acting more like a boy of his young age should. Harriet had been a godsend for his family. And James loved her dearly. "Uncle Buck is waiting outside with our horses," he said impatiently, as he peered out the window.

"I'm coming, Son. Give me a moment." James strode over to Mrs. Brady and handed Adam to her. He went to Harriet and kissed her forehead. Then did the same for Pearl. He left the baby in peace as he didn't want to disturb her feed.

Mrs. Brady stood nearby with young Adam in her arms. She'd offered to help for a few months after the baby was born, to ease Harriet's burden. James wondered if he could impose on her when their next child arrived—in a little over seven months. She was even more like a grandmother than a housekeeper now. She seemed to have found her happy place with the youngsters—just as she did when Will and Pearl were young.

His life, and that of his family, had changed dramatically when he married Harriet. She might have been a complete stranger when they married, but Harriet quickly became part of the family. James knew Anna would be content knowing they were now alright. Her children were being loved, along with her husband. And finally, the empty rooms were finally being filled. Not to mention the laughter that filled the house.

James had no regrets, and his children had no aftereffects of that dreadful day when they were taken hostage. Praise God.

"Let's go, Will," James finally said, as he glanced back at the picture before him. His heart was filled with love and joy, and he couldn't ask for anything more.

Thank you so much for reading my book – I hope you enjoyed it.

I would greatly appreciate you leaving a review where you purchased, even if it is only a one-liner. It helps to have my books more visible!

Multi-published, award-winning and bestselling author Cheryl Wright, former secretary, debt collector, account manager, writing coach, and shopping tour hostess, loves reading.

She writes both historical and contemporary western romance, as well as romantic suspense.

She lives in Melbourne, Australia, and is married with two adult children and has six grandchildren. When she's not writing, she can be found in her craft room making greeting cards.

Website: *http://www.cheryl-wright.com/*

Facebook Reader Group:
https://www.facebook.com/groups/cherylwrightauthor/

Join My Newsletter:

https://cheryl-wright.com/newsletter/
(and receive a free book)